SHERIFF CHANCY ROSMAN

A CHANCY ROSMAN WESTERN ADVENTURE
BOOK 1

Russell J. Atwater

Contents

Chapter 1
The New Stranger in Town

Death has been known to have his favorites, following in the footsteps of those who make his work easy, those who supply the bodies quickly and plentifully. Lennie Aldridge was one of those men. Never an outlaw, not quite.

He'd put food on his table and lined his pockets by straddling the line of the law, solving the problems of the wealthy for the right price and the blind eye of the sheriff. In 1881 Elkhorn, Nebraska, Lennie Aldridge was a man folks didn't want to see. Even more so, he was a man folks didn't want to be seen by.

Many a man had stared into the scarred, leering face of Aldridge, the cold eyes the last vision before death claimed another soul.

That afternoon, Aldridge sauntered into the mercantile, dusty and irritated as usual. The scar that tore across his cheek from the corner of his mouth did little more than highlight the grim expression he typically bore. "Boy!" he hollered, ignoring the woman approaching the cash register.

Andy Nichols was twelve, old enough to hold down the store when needed, and more than versed in the unspoken codes of the west. The most important in Elkhorn was that one did not cross Lennie Aldridge. He caught the woman's eye, nodding ever so slightly to acknowledge her before turning to the man. "Sir?"

"There's a horse tied up out there. The one with that fancy saddle on it. Go find me the owner and tell 'im I'm fixin' to buy it."

"I'm not sure if he's—"

"I ain't askin' you nothin'. I'm tellin' you. Find me the man who owns that horse."

"Yes, sir." Andy turned to the woman. "It'll be just a moment…"

"Get!" Aldridge hollered, stamping his boot on the floor and swatting at Andy with his hat as the boy hurried by.

Aldridge turned back to the woman, letting his eye wander over her without any sense of shame or propriety, assessing her much like he had the saddle just moments before.

***

Two doors down, Andy burst into the town's main restaurant, Addie's Fine Meals. He knew perfectly well who the horse and saddle belonged to. He also knew Chancy Rosman wasn't a man who took to being told what to do.

Or at least that's what he felt.

Rosman had ridden into town early that morning, just as Andy had opened the shop. The man had been after tobacco and bullets, not an uncommon shopping list for the cowboys in the burg, but through his years in the store, Andy had gained the ability to read folks.

Some were all bluster and some were timid and unaware. Some folks acted as if they could ignore their troubles and they would go away.

Chancy Rosman was none of these.

The way he held himself. The way he eyed the room. Even the comfortable saunter and hang of the gun belt. Andy read confidence and an iron will in Rosman.

Andy could be the messenger—there was no fear in that when taking news to a man like Chancy—but the man who sent this particular message was likely to be less than pleased with the response.

Andy scanned the dining hall, slightly unnerved to realize that, by the time he spotted Chancy, the man's eyes were already upon him, as if waiting. "Sir," Andy said, walking over to the small table. "I apologize for interrupting your breakfast. I know that's ungentlemanly. But, well, you see…"

Rosman settled back in his chair, pushing out the empty seat across from him with his boot. "Settle in, kid. No need to get excited this early in the morning."

Andy hesitated, then sat, speaking more to the remains of egg yolks on the plate than to the gunslinger. "Your horse, sir. You left him—"

"Her."

"Her, hitched up outside the mercantile."

"I did." Chancy sipped at a chipped mug of coffee. "Everything all right?"

"Yes, yes, sir," Andy stumbled on his words.

"Hey," Chancy leaned forward, catching the kid's eye across the table. "Me and you ain't got no beef. Just tell me what you come to tell me, and we'll see what we gotta do about it."

"It's Lennie Aldridge," Andy said.

"I'm afraid that name don't mean much to me, kid. But judging by the way you say it, I reckon it's supposed to."

"He's, well…" Andy swallowed with a dry throat. "They say he's just here to keep some order, but I don't know…" The kid trailed off, unsure how much of the local common knowledge it was appropriate to share with an out-of-towner, even if the man was walking into trouble.

"I think I know the type," Chancy said. "What I don't know is what this fella's got to do with me and my horse."

"Actually, it's your saddle," the boy said. "He wants to buy it."

"Oh, well shoot." Chancy smiled, leaning back in his chair. "You should've said something sooner, kid. That problem's easily solved. Saddle ain't for sale."

Andy sighed, looking back at the dark-stained wood of the table. "It ain't to your health to say no to Lennie Aldridge, sir, if I may say so."

"You may say whatever ya like, kid. I ain't gonna fight ya over it. But I'll tell ya what, seeing as how you don't look too keen on being the bearer of this news, you tell your man Eldson—"

"Aldridge."

"Him too." Chancy grinned. "You tell him I said to come on down and meet me at the saloon and we can have a little chat like adults, instead of sending messengers out when them boys is trying to earn an honest wage."

Andy looked up at him.

"All right," Chancy said. "Just tell him to come down to the saloon. You can leave off that last part."

"Yes, sir." The boy hopped from his chair, eager to get back to the store, back to his customers, and done with any business having to do with Lennie Aldridge. "Thank you, sir."

"I ain't done nothin' for ya, kid," Chancy laughed. "Thank you for the head's up."

Andy nodded and ran back out onto the dusty street.

***

Aldridge was just lifting the saddle off the uneasy Appaloosa when he heard Andy's footsteps behind him. Irritated at only hearing the running boy and not the steps of the horse's owner, he dropped the saddle back down and turned, quickly drawing his gun from the holster.

The boy skidded, lost his footing, and hit the dirt. "It's just me, Mr. Aldridge! Don't shoot!"

Suppressing a grin, Aldridge held a bead on the boy just a moment longer, then slowly slid the gun back home on his hip.

"You best learn not to come up on a man like that, boy. You find most folks aren't so keen to think before they shoot."

"Yes, sir." Andy got to his feet, dusting himself off.

"Now, where is he?" Aldridge spat in the dust at the boy's feet.

"He was just finishing up breakfast, sir, said to meet him—"

The back of Aldridge's hand met the side of the boy's head, knocking him back to the dirt. "Did I tell you to go find his diary and let me know every doggone thing he's doing?"

"No, sir." Andy stayed down this time, out of arm's length.

"What'd I say?"

"To bring him back, sir. And I tried." Andy scuttled a few feet back, just barely dodging the tip of Aldridge's boot as he kicked out at the boy. "He said to meet him in the saloon."

"You ain't worth a bucket of pig guts, you know it?" The man spit again. "Get outta my way."

Aldridge stomped off down the road. The sound of Andy's hurried steps back to the perceived safety of the store bringing a bitter smile to his face.

***

Inside the Horseshoe Saloon, Chancy Rosman leaned on the bar, talking to an acquaintance. As the batwing doors burst open, banging off the inner walls of the room, he glanced up into the long mirror running the length of the bar.

The man in the doorway was rangy, lanky, and filthy. He held himself like someone who'd rather throw a punch than talk, and Rosman had a good guess he'd just found his prospective customer.

"Who might this fella be?" Rosman said in a low tone to the man next to him.

His friend glanced up at the mirror. "That's your boy," he said. "I'm tellin' ya though, Chancy, don't get tangled up with this one."

"Don't look like so much to me."

"It ain't him ya gotta worry about. He's one of McFarland's boys. 'Bout the only one McFarland needs, from the way I've heard it told. One trigger-happy son of a gun, right there."

"Yeah, he looks it." Chancy turned to face the room, leaning back on the bar, his elbows up. "Let's see what kinda show he's looking to put on for us."

Rosman's friend turned, glanced back at Aldridge, and kept his seat. "I'm telling you, let it be. Aldridge'll put a bullet in your heart. McFarland just likes to tie a loose rope around your neck and watch you strangle a bit more each day."

"Sounds like I need to come up with a third option."

"Just don't cause trouble, Chancy."

"Wouldn't dream of it."

At the appearance of the hired gun, the room had grown quiet.

Aldridge was known throughout the town and county as unpredictable and wild. With the strength of Frank McFarland at his back, the folks knew to tread lightly till the man gave some sign of what he was thinking. Even then, that often wasn't much.

Cold-blooded, yes, calculating, yes, but shifty and manipulative, too. More than one man had met his demise when a handshake with Aldridge ended with a bullet in the belly.

Aldridge looked around the room, waiting for quiet. His face was smug, cocky. He found his favorite targets, the men who avoided him at all costs or kowtowed to his whims, and glared them down, finding great amusement in knowing they feared him.

"I's lookin' for the man who owns that 'Loosa hitched up outside the mercantile," he said finally. His gravelly voice was loud, cutting through any remaining hushed tones and drawing the room to complete silence.

Chancy could hear the clop of horse hooves out in the street, voices in the distance. But in the Horseshoe, not a board creaked. He sized up the man. A fellow who had to yell to get his voice heard: that was one kind, the usual kind, of bully. A man who was quiet, a man who made you lean in to hear because he wasn't making a spectacle of himself. That was a different sort altogether.

Chancy decided to watch a moment longer.

Aldridge glared around the room, the silence apparently only adding fuel to his anger. "So nobody knows who it is, huh? Just some horse showed up out of the blue?" He looked up at the bar, his eyes landing on the unfamiliar visage of Chancy Rosman.

A slight gleam came to his dark eyes. "I guess I'll have to go talk to my pal Andy then. Seems he must've given me some wrong information. Nothing a tanned hide won't solve."

Chancy met the man's gaze, patient. Watching.

To the town regulars, nothing in particular seemed to change. But the air became electric. One could almost feel the agitation growing inside Aldridge as the seconds ticked by and they left his demand unanswered.

And now, his threat seemed to fall on deaf ears as well. His hands fidgeted, fingers jumping on and off the butt of his revolver, desirous to act but yet somehow uncertain.

The eyes of the hired gun never moved, though. They focused solely on one man.

Finally, Chancy spoke. "No need to go bother the kid," he said. "He told me what you was after. I told 'im to send ya here. His part's done I reckon."

"Well…" Aldridge looked around the room, arms spread dramatically. "Look at that. So everybody ain't deaf and dumb in here. Just stupid." The act of speaking seemed to return him to some kind of balance.

Chancy watched him from the bar. Men like this were unpredictable. Their words gave them confidence. Men like this found a role and played it well. Unfortunately, part of that role was to be slippery, and Chancy kept a keen eye on the man's hands.

"I'm takin' that saddle off your hands," Aldridge said, walking across the room.

"That a fact?"

"I was fixin' to pay right well for it too," Aldridge said, "but seein' as how you saw fit to drag me all the way down here and play hide 'n' seek, the price's been droppin'."

Chancy looked at him, letting the man ramble on.

"Folks around here think I can be a tough man to deal with," Aldridge said, enjoying his audience. "And I tell ya, I don't know why I gotta be the bad guy in that situation. All I ask is folks be reasonable, and I be reasonable right back. So how's… oh… ten dollars sound for that saddle?"

Chancy looked around the room. The sum was paltry, a number set to make a man refuse.

"Tell you what," Chancy said. "These folks don't wanna listen to us haggle. Let's step outside and have us a chat."

An eager glint flashed in Aldridge's eyes. "That happens to be my preferred way to do business."

All pretense of negotiation dropped. Aldridge taunted the man as they walked out into the street, slowly angling away from one another. "I'm being reasonable," he said loudly, ensuring that, should anyone ask, it was clear his offer had been refused, that the gunfight wasn't his idea.

"Thing is," Chancy said, "that saddle came from a man I got a high regard for. He gave it to me on account of my saving his daughter a while back, so it's got what you might call a good memory to it. And truth be told, I just don't want somebody like you dirtying it up." He stopped in the street, looking down at the hired gun.

Aldridge paused, unused to this kind of backtalk. "Seems to me it don't matter what you want, stranger. Only one of us'll be riding out today. Looks like I'll be getting me that Appaloosa to boot."

"Last chance," Rosman said, adjusting his hat to block the sun.

Aldridge grinned, his sneer pulling back to reveal yellowed teeth. "I think you'll find—" and that was when he went for his gun. It was a dirty trick, a distraction, but one that always worked.

The crack of the gunshot split the still air, and Aldridge looked down, confused.

He had distracted his foe. He'd gone for his gun. He'd heard the shot. But his revolver was still holstered. A warmth ran down his stomach. He had time to register the red splotch on his chest before falling to his knees, then face down in the dusty main street.

Chapter 2
The Notorious
Frank McFarland

Earlier that morning, in his office above the Horseshoe Saloon, Frank McFarland sat at his desk. The morning light poured through the tall windows behind him, illuminating piles of papers, ledger books overflowing with numbers, and various stacks of gold and silver coins used as paperweights for small bundles of currency.

McFarland sweated freely in the midmorning heat, his bulk in no way adding to the comfort he felt out in the Nebraska summers. If it had been up to him, he'd have moved the whole operation up toward the Dakotas, over into the fertile ground of Colorado or the Wyoming territory. Even farther north in the state itself would've been preferable.

But business didn't run on comfort. In fact, he'd found the more uncomfortable he could make his clients, often the better things went in the long run. Besides, with Elkhorn sitting on the Missouri River, there wasn't a better spot for miles around to enact the negotiations he had in mind.

Already the money had been coming in easily, freely. As if the folks out this way were happy to give it to him.

With the only other option coming in the form of Lennie Aldridge, though, he supposed they were.

He ran his stubby finger down a column of numbers, calculating on a sheet of paper beside him. He reached into a drawer at his knee and pulled out a plat map, plots lightly shaded dotting much of the county.

Checking his papers again, he took the short pencil and gently colored in three more areas on the map, not enough to obscure any of the vital information noted but enough to tell him the one thing he really cherished the map for.

He held it up in front of him, eyes scanning the outline of the county, the clumps of darker areas, and the empty spaces where nothing valuable could—or likely ever would—be built.

Every county had its scrub areas, just like every town had its down-and-out districts. But with some creative ingenuity, McFarland planned on vitalizing every square mile on the map, even if it was only for a paper company. He smiled to himself, noting the freshly shaded areas. He now owned more than half the county.

McFarland leaned back in his chair, the springs squeaking a tired protest as he laced his fingers behind his head and thought about his next moves. Owning the land was one step.

It was important, after all, especially in the rapid growth of the great United States, where having a plot of land was considered the true sign of citizenship, patriotism, and loyalty to God and country.

What Frank had found, though, was that most folks were more than happy to lease land, to rent it even if it got them in a house, gave them a garden to work, and kept them busy and involved. If he owned the land that house sat on, well, all the better for him.

Nothing turns the screws on a man like the fear of being out in the cold.

Of course, McFarland wasn't all bad. He'd be happy to tell anyone so himself. In fact, several investments outside of real estate were practically legal.

Granted, creative bookkeeping was something he considered more of a skill than a detriment. After all, if he was smart enough to find a loophole in a system, didn't it give him the right to take advantage of it? It wasn't his fault people created faulty regulations that were just waiting for a man of his skills.

If someone had wanted a watertight set of laws, the first group they should've asked, in his opinion, was the lawbreakers. Anyone can look at a dollar bill, but no one knows it as intimately as the man who's trying to copy it.

Thankfully, he'd been able to get away from the riskier activities of questionable legality and now stood firmly, straddling the line, one foot on either side. Sure, he wasn't one hundred percent honest, but who was?

If anyone wanted to review his numbers, well, the money coming in from the stockyards, the packing houses—shoot, the breweries alone—would more than explain where his money was coming from. Or at least the lumps anyone needed to know about. And given the full capacity of his rented lands, no one seemed to want to know too much at all.

No one except Travis, of course. The Honorable Gerrit Travis, mayor of Elkhorn, and royal pain in McFarland's neck.

McFarland had heard the man was tough, but he'd also never encountered a man who didn't have a price. And in his experience, the price was usually much lower than one would expect.

A secure retirement. Some extra land. Men were willing to sell their integrity for so little when the other option was to lose their livelihood, their home, or their family. In previous ventures, when he moved into town, anyone who wasn't out within the first six months had no intention of going anywhere.

They might hem and haw and raise a ruckus about many things. But to get up and go? To uproot themselves and start over again some place else? No, not too many people wanted to take that route.

So when things went to plan, McFarland had everything in place within the first year and was in a good position to pass things on to a second-in-command while he moved on to find the next goldmine. But then he'd met Mayor Travis.

At first, everything had gone swimmingly. Travis was more than pleased with the amount of money McFarland was sinking into the local economy. Everywhere McFarland went, problems were being solved.

Debts became bought, funding suddenly appeared, even agreements between rival struggling businesses had been negotiated.

What Travis didn't know, or at least at first refused to recognize, was that most of the negotiation involved Lennie Aldridge and six bullets. But that was no fault of McFarland's. He offered the simplest of choices to people: get in line, or get out.

What they choose was no concern of his, as the outcome would be the same for him. It continually surprised him that anyone took the high road. Why work your fingers to the bone when you can become part of a bigger system, which he had to admit was a booming success across the country?

But Travis was a stickler for the rules. He got curious, and curiosity was something McFarland wouldn't—couldn't—tolerate.

A voice called out from down in the street behind him. Ordinarily, that type of thing wouldn't have caught his attention. The office was, like everything in McFarland's life, something he had picked out personally, specifically.

The second-story room on the corner of the building gave him a clear view of the two main streets into Elkhorn. He could keep an eye on the businesses he owned.

He could see who was coming into or heading out of town. And he wouldn't be taken by surprise in the one place he was supposed to feel the most secure.

The general din of a town, any town, quickly moved its way into his subconscious. So much of it was the same, anyway. The sound of horse hooves. Drunken cowboys. Children. Animals. Wagons. It was all the same to him. The only thing that really changed was the address he wrote on his envelopes.

This was different, though, familiar somehow.

He stood from his chair, groaning at the strain on his knees, and moved over to the window, pulling one of the thick, red satin curtains back to the side a little more. He removed his glasses, polishing them on his vest and readjusting them on his nose.

Yes, it was what he thought he'd heard: Lennie Aldridge, at it again.

McFarland walked over to his desk and picked up a small handbell, ringing it lightly.

The door at the far side of the room opened, and a tall, red-haired woman entered. Her dress was form-fitting at the top, then blossomed into a bell over her hips and legs. Her thick, curled hair was piled up on the top of her head, leaving shining earrings on display, catching the sunlight as she made her way across the room.

He'd met her back in Indianapolis. She was the only person to ever put one over on him, and for that, rather than have her removed from the equation, he'd given her the highest position in his organization. She wasn't just smart; she was slick, elusive, and clever. And her large blue eyes were often the only tool she needed to get the job done.

"Anne-Marie," McFarland said. "Come here a moment, please. There seems to be a show going on."

The woman joined him at the window, pulling aside the other curtain. "Ah, yes," she said. "Well, this should be mildly entertaining, at least."

McFarland smiled. "For a moment, perhaps. That man is one of the best guns I've found so far. If we can get him to use his brain instead of shooting off his mouth as much as his gun, we'll be getting somewhere."

"I wouldn't hold my breath," the woman said. Her voice was low, breathy. She carried herself like a woman who did not need nor heed any man unless she knew there was a healthy payoff waiting at the end.

"You don't care for the boy much, do you?" McFarland said.

"I don't care for anyone who has to resort to this kind of nonsense and spectacle to get things done," she said.

"The code of the west, I'm afraid."

"Ha!" she tossed her head back. "A code made up by boys hoping to sound tough. What is the code of the west but an excuse to play with your guns? And don't you, of all people, tell me it's about honor."

McFarland smiled. "I'll tell you what I see down there." He pointed to Aldridge. "I see a man who didn't have any job, any home, or any direction until he met me. Now, he's loyal, he's vicious, and he doesn't stick his nose where it doesn't belong. That young man may look like a mutt, but he's a guard dog.

"Now over here," he pointed to the other man, a tall, well-built stranger. "This man, I don't know. But if I had to guess, he wandered into town, thinking he was worth more than he is. Came here expecting something he hadn't earned. He's been gambling from town to town, and the only difference it makes is that mathematics has no feelings. His time will run out. And were I to wager on it, I'd say the only one who doesn't know today is that day is him.

"So, honor? Code? Anne-Marie, I don't know. I know one man is showing loyalty to his employer, which could be seen as selfishness, greed. I know one man has shown up a stranger and is now in a position to kill a man he's most likely never met before. They are both damned, from a strictly biblical perspective.

"Such a beacon of hope and cheer," the woman said, smirking.

Down in the street below, the voices had hushed. At first glance, not a soul was around besides the two men standing in the road, twenty feet apart, as still as statues. As he looked closer though, McFarland could see the eyes of the townspeople.

They huddled behind barrels, peaked through windows, and crouched at the ends of buildings, wanting to protect themselves but not miss out on the spectacle of real gunfire, real danger, real blood and excitement.

From his window perch, McFarland was, he supposed, not too terribly different. Though, what he was investigating wasn't something as paltry as a cockfight or a horse race. No, he was keeping tabs on his investment.

If things went as he expected here, he'd need to find out who the stranger was, follow the back-trail, decide whether this was the beginning of trouble or, as was typically the case, another loner who spent his last moments face down in the dusty street out west.

Despite his anticipation, or perhaps because of it, McFarland was startled by the gunshot. His vision was not what it once was, and it had never been spectacular, but looking down at the street for a moment, he was unsure whether Lennie had even moved to pull his gun.

Surely the stranger couldn't be that fast?

As he and Anne-Marie watched, Lennie went down to his knees, falling forward into the dust, motionless.

McFarland looked at the woman next to him. She was expressionless, neither amusement nor disappointment on her face. Her mouth was a thin line.

"It would appear you need a new gunman," she said.

"Did he even attempt to draw?"

Anne-Marie was the only person who knew about McFarland's eyes. It was a confidence he was not pleased with but one that had proven necessary as they'd worked together more closely. With most things, no one would ever notice, but in moments like this—fast motion, distance—he could never be sure.

"He started to," she said, her tone flat. "Didn't even clear the holster, though, from what I could tell. That man, Frank, whoever he is, that man is fast."

"You don't recognize him?"

"He's new to me, but I don't keep tabs on every cowboy who rides through town. It is possible that he came in early this morning. He hasn't been hanging about any of the usual spots, though."

"I see." McFarland rubbed his chin, moving away from the window and back to his chair. The sunlight coming through the glass was hot, and he was tired of standing, staring at a dead employee in the road.

Someone would have to take care of the body, and given Aldridge's lack of relations, that someone would likely be him. It was the contradiction of gunfighters: the less attached they were, the better, but when they were done, it all fell back in the employer's lap.

"Want me to find out who he is?" Anne-Marie asked, moving toward the door.

"Yes," he started. "But don't trouble yourself. Send Tillman over. If this man's new in town, he may think they actually need to talk to him about shooting down one of our own."

"I don't think that plan's gonna work too good." She smiled.

"Look, Anne-Marie, I know you don't care for the men I've hired here, but you've been with me long enough to know the most important thing—this is passing. Tillman may be a good-for-nothing drunk, but he's the one who was appointed sheriff, so as far as that man's concerned, Tillman is the one who ought to talk to him.

Let's see if the law spooks him at all. See what kind of mettle he has. Then if he seems worth it, you can have your pass at him. But remember, we are here *temporarily.* You can't nix every man that comes needing work just because you don't like them."

She eyed him patiently from the door. "Anything else, *sir*?"

McFarland sighed, looking at the papers on his desk, knowing he needed to trust the woman, knowing that's why he'd hired her in the first place, but also knowing he hated it when she was right.

"Fine," he said. "Check on Tillman first. If he's less than half in the bottle, let him do his thing. If he's passed out in his own drunk tank again, well, I'll come up with something else."

"And if he's neither?"

"What else could he be? It's Tillman. There are only the two states."

"There is a third, Mr. McFarland, one which I was intending to tell you about before our diversion on Main Street."

"And what's that?"

"He's dead, sir."

"What?"

"Gunned down last night over Gretna way. Seems like your boys are running thin."

McFarland slammed his hands on his desk. "Go, Anne-Marie," he snarled. "I'll ring for you when I need you."

Chapter 3
Mayor Gerrit Travis

Meanwhile, across town, Mayor Gerrit Travis was looking out his office window, running his hands through his thinning hair, and having a very similar conversation with his secretary, Jane Whitman.

"I suppose it had to happen eventually," he said, "though I kept banking on later."

"Everyone has his time, sir," Jane said from across the desk.

"Was he drunk?" He paused. "What kind of question is that? I assume he was drunk."

"Yes," she replied, "I believe so. At least, I know the gunfight was outside the saloon in Gretna, so it stands to reason…"

"Maybe I should just be thankful it happened outside of Elkhorn," the mayor mused. "Saves us at least a bit of the trouble. I should've never given him the job, but I kept thinking he'd come around."

"And it's what the people wanted." Jane looked down as if even she didn't really believe what she'd just said.

"Yes, yes. So it would appear, at least. And perhaps that's the bright side of all of this," he caught himself. "Not that I'm glad he, or anyone, met his maker in the middle of a street, but..." He pulled a drawer open on his desk, rummaging for a sheet of paper. "The one thing that we know for sure is we need a new sheriff, even if just temporarily. Perhaps solely temporarily. If we play our cards right, perhaps we can give a few fellows a run at it and see how things go before we find ourselves in the same situation again."

"You think *he*'ll let that happen?"

Both the mayor and his secretary knew how much influence McFarland carried in town since shortly after his arrival and subsequent land grab, though neither liked to admit it. In some ways, the man felt like a necessary evil. While his motivations and schemes weren't always pure, the outcomes were often to the good of all, even if at the cost of a few.

Still, Travis hated the setup. Since McFarland's arrival, Travis had spent many a night at his desk, thinking around corners, looking for loopholes. But the man never quite got his hands dirty. McFarland was the worst kind of criminal: a smart one who convinced others to do his bidding without ever becoming involved in any way that would implicate himself criminally.

"I can't imagine he would like it if the people actually elected the new sheriff," Travis said. "But that might be just the angle we need. If we appoint a sheriff temporarily, we should still be in the clear. The post will be technically open and, once the proper man has established himself, it would be a fairly smooth transition to just leave him where he is.

We could allow suggestions and input from the townsfolk, but I'd just about bet, once we have a trustworthy, reliable man on the job, there won't be enough steam to get him booted out."

"But there's always that chance."

"You're quite right, Miss Whitman." The mayor scanned the list of names in his hand. "I want you to look through this list over the next few days. I can't say I've got a great feeling about any of them, if I'm to be frank, but maybe something will come to you."

"Potentials?"

He sighed. "I guess one could call them that. They're all decent men, but that goes for most of the citizens here. We've been lucky to end up with the folks we have. But this job is going to call for something a little more particular than just keeping everyone toeing the line. Most of our people do that on their own. We need someone with a little more gumption if we're going to solve all our problems."

"I…" The secretary looked at the mayor, trailing off.

"Go ahead." He gestured toward her. "I hired you because I trust your insights, Miss Whitman. Always speak freely, even if you think I won't like it. Perhaps especially when you think that."

"It just sounds like you're wanting someone who will take down McFarland. And I don't know how well that will go over. As you said, some things he's done, well, to be honest, they've been good for the town."

"I completely agree. The thing is, though, it's the way he does them. The way he achieves his ends. Yes, they are faster. And yes, the profits are often larger than we could manage on our own. But as my grandmother always said, patience is a virtue."

"Mine always said, 'A bird in the hand is worth two in the bush,' and I think we might have many people who lean more toward my grandmother than yours."

"That I don't doubt," the man said. "But sometimes one just has to grit one's teeth and bear a situation. We want to get folks looking toward the future of Elkhorn, not just the next payday."

"I couldn't agree more, sir. I'm simply stating what I think most folks feel. You and I are in a steady position. Others… many don't have it so well."

"Yes…" the mayor looked down at his hands. "That's part of the west, I'm afraid. It's not for everyone. But that doesn't mean we simply take the easiest option. In fact, it means we shouldn't. Life out here isn't easy, not yet, anyway. And as folks keep moving toward the other ocean, it's just going to get tougher. But we can make Elkhorn a safe place to be. A good place."

Jane smiled at the man. His dedication to service, his undying optimism. They were reasons she'd been so pleased to accept the job. He was realistic, but he never lost his hope. "So, what exactly am I looking for in this temporary sheriff?" she asked.

The mayor steepled his fingers, looking up at the ceiling. "Sometimes I think it's just going to be a situation where we know it when we see it," he said. "We need someone reliable, of course. And sober, which probably knocks out half our list already."

"How about reliably sober?" Jane grinned.

The mayor smiled. "That may be a good way to frame it. I can't fault a man for downing a few on his own time, but we need to keep the bottles out of the office this time. The thing that may be harder than that, though, is we need someone who isn't cowed by McFarland."

"Now that will certainly limit our options, I'm afraid."

"Yes," the man mused. "It certainly puts us in a bind. Anyone who's been here for too long has likely learned the value of tipping his hat to McFarland. Anyone fresh out of the saddle likely won't have proven himself in any way that would remotely qualify him for the job. Talk is cheap everywhere, but especially this side of the Mississippi."

"It is a temporary position, though," the lady said.

"And we never said how temporary that could be," the mayor replied. "I'd hate to put the badge on the wrong man, even for a few days, but given the situation, it may be a risk we have to take. We just have to hope any man not suited for the job will know it before someone gets hurt."

The secretary smiled. "That is the very least of my concerns. I trust your judgment before anyone else in this town. I'm sure you'll make the right choice."

Travis smiled. "I appreciate your faith in me, but you won't get off that easy. Why did you think I put you in charge of this? Getting past you is the first step in the application."

"Oh, I don't know if I…"

"Miss Whitman, I hired you because I trust you. Not because of your experience as an assistant. If you'll recall, you had none before coming here. But you're reliable, you're level-headed, and you shoot straight. If you find a man who fits those requirements, we should be well on our way. I won't hang you out to dry. The final say will be mine, naturally. But you can save me from interviewing every yahoo who's got an itchy trigger finger or a dry gullet."

Jane nodded. "I'll do my best, sir." She stood to leave the office.

"One more thing," the mayor said from his chair. "If I were you, I'd lean toward the side of… well, shall we say, tough. We don't need roughnecks, and we don't need cattle thieves, but we need a man who can pick one out of a crowd."

Jane frowned a bit. "Like he can smell his own?"

The mayor nodded his head noncommittally. "Not necessarily that. Just someone who's seen a few things and knows the signs before trouble really gets settled in. You'll do fine. Now go find me some applicants."

"Yes, sir." She smiled, hurrying back to her small desk in the outer office.

Travis watched her go. The woman was good at what she did, despite, or perhaps because of, her occasional lack of confidence in her skills. While some would view second-guessing as a shortcoming, in a position like Jane's, with the number of hard decisions that had to be made in the mayor's office every day, he needed someone who would evaluate and reevaluate, taking in situations from every angle.

The only problem was, in all his time as the mayor, even he'd never seen quite the man he was hoping to find. Unless the wind of fate blew a new saddle-toughened man his way, this could be a long and arduous process.

"Still, we never said how temporary it could be," the mayor said under his breath, returning to some other work on his desk.

Chapter 4
The Right Man
for the Job

Having spent the better part of two weeks in Elkhorn, Chancy Rosman was feeling like he'd found a place he could settle in. Or at least somewhere he wasn't planning on blowing through, like he'd done so often in his travels.

Since the unfortunate incident over the saddle, or perhaps because of it, he'd found life to be calmer here. The days went by smoothly, and he'd made acquaintances, even something close to friends, in the bustling town.

More by luck than through any particularly diligent hunting, he'd even found a calm, comfortable boarding house close to the edge of town. He liked the location, close to anything he needed to do, but far enough toward the outskirts to avoid too much bustle.

It was quiet without being secluded, relaxing without being too uneventful. What he enjoyed most, however, was the proprietress. The woman, a few years his younger, was pretty in her own way but felt more like a relative to him than a romantic conquest.

Teresa Slayton ran a tight, no-nonsense house. The expectations were clear, and the meals were excellent, two things that, in Chancy's mind anyway, were paramount in a lodging.

The woman was widowed, and while this was not an uncommon state of affairs, she bore her burden with square shoulders and a firm determination to make the best life she could. Much of this, Chancy often assumed, was because of Betsy, Teresa's eleven-year-old daughter and only child.

He'd watched the pair interact much over the days he'd been staying there and had no doubts Betsy would grow to be just as strong a woman as her mother hoped. When not at school or in her room studying, the girl was busy working somewhere, helping with meals, doing chores outside around the house, anticipating the needs of both the paying guests and her mother.

She was a smart girl, raised by a smart woman, and while Chancy had more than once offered his help, the pair seemed to find joy in their independence.

They accepted his offers only when he practically begged them or, more often than not, simply did things without mentioning it. They always caught him, of course, but the exasperated sighs of Teresa belied a quiet thankfulness at not being required to ask for help.

He often found his duties at the house relegated to after-dinner domino games with one or both of the ladies of the house. Not only did he simply enjoy the banter and fellowship, it gave him a reasonable excuse for helping out.

In this way, he could claim his motivation was to free the girls up for something he enjoyed, rather than making them feel he was helping out of pity or a need of theirs.

And the games were well worth it. The two Slaytons, while serious to an almost grimness during the days, threw themselves into their relaxation with just as much determination. More than once, when other boarders had overnighted, the trio had been hushed from the stairs by a light-sleeping guest.

Theirs was a raucous, uninhibited pleasure in one another's company, something that felt more akin to a family member than a chance friendship in the middle of a strange new town.

This particular night, perhaps feeling the same sisterly affection for the man, Teresa had once again brought up the extent of his stay in Elkhorn over cups of iced tea on the front porch after Betsy had gone up to bed.

"A man's gotta have some way of keeping himself occupied," Teresa was saying. "And you can't spend all your time sneaking around here, trying to do Betsy's work for her."

He smiled at the friendly jab. "Well, somebody's gotta let the poor girl relax every once in a while."

Chancy put his feet up on the porch railing, tipping his chair back on two legs. "Her mother is a real taskmaster."

Teresa swatted his arm with her free hand. "Maybe you just haven't seen a day of work in too long. Traipsing about from town to town, taking whatever comes your way until there's enough to move on to the next place."

"Perhaps I'm just a particular type of fella," he said, looking out into the dark.

"Peculiar, maybe."

He laughed. "You might have a point there. But I like my life. When I want to settle, I'll settle. For now…" He ended with a shrug.

"Deke was the same way," Teresa said. "Bless his soul. That man had the itchiest feet I've ever seen. But I'll tell you one thing: there wasn't an evening he didn't make it back to Betsy and me. Day trips for this and that, though, Lord, I couldn't even count. He always said he was lucky to find a wife with such patience, but I think he was even luckier to find a horse with such endurance."

"Lucky twice over then," Chancy mused. "You are an excellent woman, Teresa. I haven't even known you for two weeks yet, but of that, I have no doubt."

"Oh, stop. I just do what a woman or any person should."

"That may very well be. I have a question for you, though."

"Oh?"

"Think you can find me a horse like that? Mine's got a bit of an attitude problem after a few day's ride."

She swatted at him again. "You are a real piece of work, Chancy Rosman. If I still had that horse, I'd be half tempted to put you on it and run him right out of town."

He laughed. "You'd do no such thing. You're still behind in the dominos tournament, and we both know you couldn't stand to see me go with the record standing as it is."

"You know me well, sir," she said. "But don't forget, I'm getting to know you well, too. And this seems like just the type of thing you'd bring up to avoid what I was talking about a moment ago. So, what exactly are your plans?"

Chancy sipped at his tea and shook his head slightly. "I've always been honest with you, with everybody, so I hope you believe me when I say I have no plans at all. I like it here. The town seems pleasant, and I like you and Betsy. Other than that, I find it rarely pays to think too far ahead."

"But something that pays might be nice," she said.

"Oh, I have little concern in that area, at least not for the time being. My mother and you would've gotten along well. She raised me to be smart, responsible... keep an eye on myself and my finances. I'm not afraid to work."

"You've made that abundantly clear," Teresa said. "That's why I find it so interesting you choose to do it here, for free, as if it's a secret."

He shrugged. "I just do what I do."

There was a moment's pause as the two settled back in their chairs, looking up at the stars in the dark night sky, listening to the sounds of the town getting itself arranged for the evening.

"You know," Chancy said, "another man might not pick up on what you're getting at here. But you've always been honest with me as well, at least as far as I can see. So spill it, Teresa. What's on your mind? Surely it's more than just dreaming about what I could do. That list is as long as the day."

"Well, it may be nothing at all, but I want you to just listen. Then I'll at least feel better for having said something."

Rosman sat his glass on the porch beside his chair. "By all means."

"Now I don't know for sure how true this is, but given the state of things and the source, I'm inclined to believe it's very much reliable. But a dear friend of mine, Jane Whitman…"

"The mayor's assistant?"

"That's the one."

"You've mentioned her a time or two. And I don't mean to cut you off here, but I'm not really the type of guy who sits well behind a desk. Office work isn't exactly my cup of tea, either."

"It's not that at all. Well, at least not entirely. Around the time you got to town, actually the very day if memory serves me, our sheriff was killed."

"I recall. Over in Gretna, wasn't it? From what I've heard, you didn't lose too much there."

"Hush, you," Teresa said. "Maybe Gerome wasn't the best man for the job. Heaven knows he felt more comfortable on a bar stool than in his desk chair, but we all have our struggles to contend with. And no one deserves that kind of death."

Chancy resettled himself in his seat. The two had never specifically talked about his run-in with Lennie Aldridge, not because it was a secret necessarily, but because it just didn't seem to come up.

Chancy had seen this kind of response in folks before. Not that Teresa feared him. She didn't see him as a murderer, especially given the situation he'd found himself in. And often, this led others to view him as a protector of sorts. A person others knew would do what needed to be done, even when the task was more than unpleasant.

The tumblers fell into place for Rosman.

"And you think I should take a shot at being the sheriff, huh? Is that where we're going?"

"Well," the woman said, "actually, yes. I see no reason you shouldn't apply for the job. Jane says the position is temporary so you won't have to feel tied down or stuck here if you decide to wander off. But for another, as things stand now, we're just lucky nothing of account has happened while the position has been empty."

"What have they been doing?"

"Looking for men, of course. But Jane says the mayor is very particular about this job."

"I mean, what have they been doing about there being no sheriff?"

"That's the thing, Chancy. Folks are getting by all right, but you and I both know it's just a matter of time before we need someone, and no one is there. And I just hate to think that, should that time come, I'll be sitting at dinner with just the man who could've been there, who should've been there but wasn't."

Chancy tipped his chair back down on all four legs, folding his hands under his chin. "You make a rather dramatic, if not wholly accurate, point."

"And just where am I being inaccurate?"

"Who says I'm the man for the job? Who says I'm the person this town needs? Maybe folks won't take to me like you and Betsy have. Maybe I'd just make a mess of the whole thing."

"And maybe a twister'll flatten the town tomorrow. Maybes are easy to come by, but hard to rely on."

"I may not be much better."

"You know that is just patently untrue. And I'm not the one taking applications, anyway. All I'm asking is that you think about it. Now it's getting late, I've said my piece, and what you do is up to you. But I'm asking you not just as a person in this town but as your friend to consider it. Really consider it."

Chancy leaned down and grabbed his glass, then offered his hand to the young woman, helping her up. "I can't very well say no to that kind of request then, can I?"

"Precisely why I worded it that way," Teresa said, hiding a small smile.

"You're a real piece of work," he laughed. "I'll lock up. You get to bed."

"And?"

"And I'll start considering," he said, following her into the boarding house.

***

Around noon the next day, Chancy was back in Abbie's Fine Meals, eating lunch. Much like with Teresa, the owner of the eatery seemed to view Chancy as less of a threat and more of a protection policy in the establishment.

After the efficient though obviously necessary way he'd dealt with Lennie, the clientele had become a little more polite, a little more respectable whenever he was around. Annie herself had said nothing specific about it, but a surprising number of coffees and meals had mysteriously been taken care of for him without a greenback leaving his wallet.

Not wanting to come across as an enforcer, Chancy had done his best to be friendly with the townspeople, especially in the places he frequented most, and overall, he'd been accepted, if only warily by some.

Everyone knew death was a part of life, and folks in these fringe towns—even the more settled ones—were aware they ran a higher risk than those back east. Even with Chancy's joviality and amiable smile, his frame was something to be reckoned with, and now that they'd seen the speed of his hand, few were keen to cross him.

Still, often as not, he'd often sit alone at one of the tables. This night he was initially pleased when he saw a man approach, gesturing to the empty chair next to him.

It took a second before Chancy could place the face, having never met the man personally, but when he made the connection, he broke into a broad smile. "Speak of the devil, and he shall appear," he said, reaching out to shake the fellow's hand. "The mayor himself. Pleasure to meet you, sir."

"Mr. Rosman," Travis said, shaking the offered hand and sitting down, "the pleasure is all mine. Or at least, I sincerely hope it to be."

"Right down to business, eh?"

"This town will not run itself. I'm a straight-shooter, and I hear the same about you. I see no need to muck things up by beating around a bush."

"Man after my own heart," Chancy said. "But it is dinnertime. Can I at least entice you to eat? Or forgive me if I do so myself? Elkhorn's got a genuine treasure in Annie here."

"I couldn't agree more, but thank you, no. I'm afraid the mayor's office doesn't allow for many long, leisurely lunches."

"Who's gonna stop you?" Chancy laughed.

"Only me," the mayor said.

"Good answer. Well, I won't be a waste of your time then, at least not intentionally. I can talk and eat. What's on your mind, sir?"

"Mr. Rosman," the mayor started.

"Chancy'll do."

"Thank you. Chancy, it's no big secret we've been running Elkhorn without much of a captain at the rudder, so to speak, law-wise for the last few weeks. I hear you've been around most of that time, and if your reputation is accurate, I imagine you've noticed much of this without me needing to tell you."

"I've heard," Chancy said. "Though I gotta say, most folks wouldn't notice. You've got a tight ship here, mostly anyway."

"This is the west," the mayor said. "Some things are bound to happen. If you're concerned about your encounter with Mr. Aldridge, I can assure you there are dozens of people more than ready to stand by your side on that. I have no concern about the matter. At least, not in any legal way."

"I see," Chancy said, leaning back in his chair.

"Yes, I've been told you do, and that's exactly what I'm looking for. I don't believe I need to spell anything out for you here. My secretary is good friends with Mrs. Slayton, and well, word gets around this town as if it were a quarter the size sometimes. I assume you know where this is going."

"I do," Chancy said. "Mrs. Slayton and me were just talking about this very thing not over twelve hours ago. And I feel your pain, Mr. Mayor, I really do. The only thing that makes me wonder is just what about me makes you think I've got any interest in the job? Shoot, for all you know, I'm on the run and simply hiding out here till things blow over somewhere else."

"Mr. Rosman, if it appeases you, I'll simply ask. Is there any legal reason I shouldn't want you as my new sheriff?"

"Legal reason? No, sir. Not any I can think of."

"I'm told you're honest, so until you prove otherwise, I'll take you at your word. You seem like the kind of man who still sees the value in that particular currency."

Chancy nodded.

"Now then, as far as your interest in the job is concerned, I suppose I would simply appeal to what I'd wager is a moral imperative in you. Perhaps the impression you've made on Mrs. Slayton and, through her, my assistant Miss Whitman wouldn't be enough. And perhaps the stories I've heard of your dealing with Aldridge, your attempts to defuse the situation, your what some might call reluctance in pulling the trigger… well, often stories are embellished. But the two of those things together, they make a strong case for an upright man who does what's right simply because it is right. Am I off the mark here?"

Chancy sipped at his water, looking off over the man's shoulder at the bustle of the lunch crowd. "No, sir. I don't reckon you're too far off the mark at all."

"Excellent. So that changes the question slightly, then. It's not a matter so much of why you would be interested in the job. It's who you are. Now it's a question of why you wouldn't be or, perhaps, what I can do to move you from where you are sitting now to a chair down the street behind the sheriff's desk. The pay is more than reasonable, the work is steady, and the impact is valuable. You would be a respected man in this town."

"Are you implying I'm not already?" Chancy grinned.

The mayor smiled. "Fair enough. But you don't strike me as a man swayed by money, so I'm simply laying this opportunity before you. It's not always a pleasant job, but it's a job that needs to be done, and I believe you're the type of man who sees the propriety in that."

"Mr. Mayor, I gotta be honest with you. If you'd tried to sell it to me any other way, I'd have told you to kick rocks, that I ain't your man. In fact, I'd just about decided to tell you that as soon as you sat down. With all due respect, of course." He smiled. "But now, see, you come in, and you talk like a man who knows what he's saying. You talk like you've got a brain in your head and are actually looking to do something in this town. So I'll tell you what. I'll think on it. I'm not gonna promise you one way or the other just yet, but I give you my word to give this some good, hard consideration."

The mayor sighed. "I'd be lying if I didn't say that's not precisely the response I came in here hoping for."

Chancy shrugged, holding his open hands out in front of him.

"But it is clearly an honest answer, and that's the most I can ask for," Travis continued. "I'll tell you this, and perhaps it'll sweeten the deal a bit. Then I'll leave you to your meal. The thing with this current opening is that it is a temporary position. If you're not pleased with the job after a reasonable amount of time, then simply say so, and I'll be back to looking for a more permanent replacement."

"Or if you aren't pleased with me."

"To be frank, yes. Though if you're half of what I've heard so far, I don't foresee that being an issue."

"Talk's pretty cheap out this way."

"My sentiments exactly." The mayor stood, reaching out for a parting handshake. "But I trust my gut, and my gut's telling me you're the man for the job. Think hard on it, Chancy, and come find me when you've decided. Until I hear otherwise, the job is yours for the taking."

"A bold move."

"Fortune favors the bold."

Chancy smiled, nodded, and watched the man walk back out into the street.

He'd been chewing on the idea ever since Teresa had brought it up, and his major concern had just been addressed. The sheriff might be the law, but that also meant he was a servant to the people.

In any job, a man was a servant to someone, and Chancy Rosman wasn't a man who enjoyed being beholden to anyone. He enjoyed his freedom, cherished it. That didn't keep him from helping others, but it allowed him to choose when and how he wanted to do that. This would be a rather different kettle of fish.

But the mayor was a no-nonsense man, and that was something to consider. In the meantime, he needed to get down to the mercantile and pick up a few things for Teresa and Betsy. They didn't know this, of course, but if he'd played his cards right, he'd be able to sneak them into the pantry while the ladies were otherwise occupied.

He left some money on the table under his plate, the foolproof way he'd found to pay in the restaurant, and headed out into the sun.

***

Like nearly every day Chancy had been in the shop, Andy Nichols was behind the counter, busy working away at some task or another. The man had asked the boy about it a time or two, given that Betsy was almost constantly in school or with her nose in a book, but the boy had always repeated the same thing. "See little need to learn about a trade when I can just stay here and learn to do one."

While it made sense, Chancy couldn't help but wish a little better for the lad. Still, it wasn't his place to meddle, and given the unpredictability of life, the boy made a good point. No need to learn to doctor if you already had a mercantile in your future.

"Howdy, friend," Chancy called as he stepped up to the counter.

"Hey, Chancy," Andy said without turning from the bins where he was sorting hardware. "How've you been?"

"Can't complain, kid, can't complain. You stayin' out of trouble?"

Andy laughed. "No time for it." He tossed a few bolts into their slot and turned, leaning on the counter in a way that mimicked Chancy's stance. "How about you?"

"As long as I see it coming, I go the other way. How's your pop?"

"Same as always. What can I do for ya today?"

"Oh…" Chancy looked around the store, running through a list in his mind. "Quite a number of things, I reckon. You got time for a delivery today? If not, I can haul it all up in a couple of trips."

"Always got the desire, if not the time," the boy said.

"Good lad. So this is what I'm thinking…" Chancy trailed off as the bell over the door rang. The boy's eyes flitted over Chancy's shoulder and, just perceptibly, widened.

Chancy straightened up to his full height, turning to see who could've caused such a reaction.

The man was scrawny and dirty, but leering in a way Chancy had seen exactly once before. "You Rosman?" the man asked.

"Maybe," Chancy said, moving slightly between the boy and the man. "Depends on who might be askin'."

"Yeah, yeah, I heard you're a tough guy," the man said. "You can drop the act. I ain't here lookin' for no trouble. Just passin' on a message. A request, I guess ya might say."

"That a fact? I suppose listening never killed nobody. Not yet anyway."

The man hitched his thumbs in his belt loops, a puzzled expression on his face as he tried to decide whether he'd just heard a threat. After a moment, he pushed his cowboy hat back and held out his hands. "All I'm here to do is tell you what I was told," he said.

"Which is?"

"Frank McFarland's waiting for you up in his office."

Chancy held the man's gaze.

"And that's it," the cowpoke said, sounding somewhat shaken. "If you're waiting on a formal invitation, you're gonna be waiting a long time. But the boss don't like to wait, so I'd be gettin' if I was you."

"Anything else?" Chancy leaned an elbow on the counter.

"I don't reckon."

"Well, all right then. Message received."

The two men eyed one another for a moment longer before the stranger backed out of the door. "I'll tell him you said that. And I'll tell him you know he don't wanna be waiting."

"You do that," Chancy said. "On your way, now."

The bell clanged again as the messenger moved back outside.

Chancy turned to Andy. "Now where were we?"

"Don't you reckon you oughtta go?" Andy asked.

Chancy sighed, folding his hands and leaning forward. "Well, Andy, you've been here longer than me. I'll leave it to your discretion. You think I oughtta be going?"

The boy shrugged. "Well, it's just… I mean, I'm not going anywhere. And folks usually jump when Mr. McFarland says so."

"You see, though, sometimes that's just the reason not to jump."

"I just know it don't pay to get him riled. And that man you shot, well…"

"I suppose I am overdue for a discussion about that." Chancy stood and patted the counter with his hands. "Well, don't you be runnin' off with some gal while I'm gone."

Andy laughed. "I'll be here."

***

The sunlight shone down in bold bars through the windows of Frank McFarland's office. Upon first entering, Chancy had noted the angle, seen out through the view McFarland would've had directly down onto the spot he'd had his run-in with Lennie Aldridge. That he was crossing paths with Aldridge's employer was something he'd expected ever since he'd been told who he'd shot.

What he didn't expect was how long it had taken. Something about such a lag didn't quite add up. Either McFarland didn't care, which to a certain extent, Chancy was sure he didn't—men like this saw others as tools, not people—or this encounter was about something else entirely.

Chancy settled into the plush chair across the desk from the man, crossed his leg over his knee, and waited.

"I believe introductions are long overdue," McFarland finally said.

Chancy shrugged, wanting to let the man talk as much as possible without giving away too much of himself.

"I assure you this unpleasantness with my former employee is nothing to be concerned about. I believe men are responsible for their decisions. Perhaps Lennie would've chosen a different course of action had he known who he was up against, but if we're being honest with one another, Mr. Rosman, I highly doubt he would've. Lennie was a hothead, and if it hadn't been your bullet that brought him down, another one would've."

Chancy nodded.

"Man of few words, I see. I appreciate that in a fellow. I especially appreciate it in my employees."

Chancy smiled. "Kind of ironic, given the situation that brought me here."

"Oh, no," McFarland said. "That is hardly the situation that brought you here. In my view, what happened between you and Lennie was simply the natural outcome of events. A mathematical probability. It's incredibly unwise, and unreasonable, for any man to carry on as if he were invincible. You simply reinforced that fact. No, there is certainly no bad blood between us, Mr. Rosman. In fact, just the opposite. From what I understand, we could have a very profitable relationship sitting here before us if we can simply come to a few terms."

"I'm sure you think so," Chancy said.

"Oh, no, Mr. Rosman, I know so. This isn't my first rodeo. Elkhorn is simply a stop on the track west. What I've done before, I'll do again. And you, my friend, have a golden opportunity to join up with me."

"That a fact?"

"I only deal in facts. There is no time for anything else.

"I see," Chancy looked around the room. "So what exactly is this relationship you foresee us beginning?"

"It's quite simple, really. From what I understand, Mayor Travis has chosen you to be the town's new sheriff."

"Temporarily," Chancy said. "We have suggested it for a temporary spell. Don't get your cart ahead of your horse."

"I think we both know the mayor wouldn't go out and invite a man to apply for a job he didn't have every intention of giving him, so I'll ignore your counterpoint for the time being."

"Great way to start things out," Chancy muttered.

"I don't have time for games and tricks. I tell you what I want, you do it, we both benefit. It's very simple."

"So let's say I take this sheriffin' job. Then what? I'm your pet lawman?"

"Oh, let's not put it so crassly. You would simply be a business associate. Perhaps I would need a favor from time to time. It would behoove me to have the assistance of someone higher up in the law enforcement area. And let's not forget, should you need a favor from time to time, I'm a man who can get many things taken care of."

"A friend with deep pockets, huh?"

"Not only deep pockets, Mr. Rosman, a wide reach as well."

"Well…" Chancy stood, cracking his back and settling his cowboy hat on his head. "Been a pleasure talking with ya, Frank, but I think I'm gonna have to pass."

"Pass?" McFarland stumbled slightly on the word, unused to being told no. "Perhaps you don't understand how this works. What I'm telling you is—"

Chancy held up a hand, silencing the man. "What you're telling me is, if I'm willing to be at your beck and call, if I'm willing to get my hands dirty to keep yours clean things might come my way. Fact is, Frank, I don't much like being at anyone's beck and call, leastwise someone I don't trust. And you, well… Let's just put it this way: the one thing it sounds like I can count on from you is that I can't count on you at all."

"You're making quite the mistake here, friend."

"No, no, I don't believe I am. Not two weeks ago, I shot one of your employees to death right outside this window." He pointed, walking over to the glass. "And I'd just about bet you sat here and watched me do it. Now you sit here and offer me a job? Says little for loyalty going both ways, as far as I can see. So before we get too carried away or I eat up anymore of what I'm sure is valuable time, I'm just tellin' ya thanks, but no thanks."

"Mr. Rosman, when you walk out that door, don't expect to walk back in. At least not of your own free will."

"See? Now that's the rub right there. I really like doing things of my own free will. So I believe I'll be exercising that will right now. See ya 'round, Frank." Chancy turned and headed for the door.

"Last chance," McFarland said. "You do not know how deep my pockets can go…"

"Or how far your reach. I got it, I got it." Chancy waved a hand behind him, exited to the outer office, and pulled the door closed.

Anne-Marie lounged in her desk chair, looking up at the man, eyes sparkling with entertainment. "He will not like that," she said, her voice low but amused.

Chancy shrugged. "Well, he's gotta get used to it eventually."

"If it is sooner," the woman said, "and you need an assistant, you let me know. McFarland's reach is wide, but mine is subtle, smooth, and well beyond what that two-bit con artist would like to believe."

"Just got a whole team of y'all in here, huh?"

Anne-Marie shrugged. "I go where it benefits me."

"That ain't a bad idea," Chancy said. He tipped his hat to the woman. "Ma'am."

***

Mayor Travis looked up from his desk at the sound of boots on the floor and a knock on the doorframe.

Chancy Rosman stood in the afternoon light. "Sir, I believe I'd like to take you up on that offer."

"Change of heart?" Travis asked.

"Just happened to come across some things could use some cleanin' up."

"Excellent," Travis said. "I'll get the papers in order. You made the right choice, Chancy."

"S'pose we'll see," Rosman said, turning to head back to the mercantile.

Chapter 5
Testing the Sheriff's Mettle

The day Chancy Rosman turned his back on Frank McFarland was the day McFarland knew it was time to tighten the noose on Elkhorn. Perhaps some would say it was an overreaction.

In McFarland's mind, however, one person daring to cross him was one too many. When that person was the new sheriff—a new sheriff who had denied one of McFarland's firm requests—well, there was no time to dawdle. A statement needed to be made, and when that moment came, McFarland loved nothing more than to make as many statements as possible, as clearly as possible, as often as possible.

Chancy's first two weeks as acting sheriff left him barely a moment behind the desk. His original plan, to ease his way into the townsfolks' minds and hearts, blew away like a tumbleweed almost the moment he pinned on his star. As if from the woodwork, a new batch of lawbreakers descended on the town.

Between gunfights, bar brawls, and theft, the town went from reasonable and controlled to lawless and unpredictable overnight. Other than seeing the inside of the sheriff's office when he brought a man in for booking and overnight behind-bars stays, Chancy rarely had a moment to set up the place to his liking.

Travis stopped in on his second day, catching Chancy between locking a man up and heading back out to calm the chaos.

"You kinda undersold this one, boss," Chancy said, turning the key in the cell door and checking the rounds in his revolver.

"I don't know what's gotten into these people," Travis said. "The blessing, I suppose, is they all seem to be unfamiliar faces. Our own people haven't turned on us, but this sudden outbreak is unprecedented."

"C'mon now, Mayor," Chancy said, "you're telling me you don't have the foggiest what's happening here?"

Travis looked at him, his jaw clenched. "I suppose I was hoping for randomness."

Chancy shrugged. "I can see your point, but when there's a snake in the grass, it's easiest to just track him down than swing about wherever you see the blades bowing."

"You sound pretty sure of yourself."

"Well, here's how I see it. You come in and talk to me one day, offer me this job, and not two hours later, I'm in McFarland's office being offered a pretty penny to look the other way when he needs me to."

"He said that explicitly?"

"Nah, not word for word. He's too slick for that. I believe he said me and him could do one another favors from time to time."

"To which you said no, of course."

"Of course. Couldn't've been more clear about it. Seems you weren't the only one underestimating things that day, though. Wish I'd known what I was setting myself up for."

"Surely you wouldn't have been, haven't been, cowed by this already?"

"Well…" Chancy settled on the desk, stealing a moment's rest. "Fact of the matter is, I'm not big on running from anything. McFarland seems to send this message especially to me. I'd bet ya a silver eagle. If I went up there and kissed his boots, a lot of this would cool off."

"But you won't."

"Not if I plan on looking at myself in the mirror anytime soon. But here's the deal, sir, you see just as well as I do. I can hold my own, but I can't be in two places, or three, at once. You said you had some other folks in mind for this job before I took it, right?"

"Well, yes, but they aren't… How should I put this…?"

"They aren't quite up to snuff is a fine way to put it. And that's all right with me. All I need is somebody who can sit at this here desk, write what needs written, and make sure them cell doors stay closed. Surely you got a warm body around this town who can handle that?"

"I'll put Miss Whitman on it as soon as I get back."

"Yeah, about that. I don't mean to be telling you how to do your job, and I'm sure she's a fine woman, but I knew you were considering me before we'd even met. I think we might be wise to play our cards as close as we can."

"Jane handles nearly all my affairs. I trust her completely." The mayor rubbed at his jaw.

"I'm sure you do. And I trust Mrs. Slayton as well, but the fact remains, the fewer people who know something, the fewer people who can talk about it. Find you a man you trust to sit in here. Give him a gun, don't give him a gun: that's none of my concern. But if we can get him set up and working, we'll have that much better of a chance of keeping him on our side when McFarland offers the deputy a deal as well."

"You know, I might have just the man."

"Good. Go find him. Don't bother telling me who he is. I'll know him when he gets here. As for now…" Chancy stood up and adjusted his gun belt. "I'm back in the fray."

"Sheriff Rosman, thank you."

"Thank me when we got things back in order. You may not wanna hear it, but from where I'm standing, this thing could still go either way."

***

A few days later, McFarland sat as usual, leaned back in his desk chair, a smug smile on his face. Anne-Marie was in the chair across from him, sipping sherry from a small crystal glass.

"Now will you agree that subtly isn't always the way to go?" the man said. "We've got this town running wild. And with what, half a dozen men?"

"Ten, to be precise. But that new sheriff means business. Any given moment, he's got four of them locked up, at least. As fast as we can get them out, another one goes in. To be blunt with you, I'm not inclined to wager on an outcome just yet."

"Hogwash, Anne-Marie. Pure hogwash. You know as well as I do that this is simply math. It's an endurance game and who do you suppose will last longer? One man or ten? Unless *Sheriff* Rosman plans on working round the clock, all we have to do is choose our moments wisely. He's only human, after all. At some point, the man will have to sleep. And with these new guns, even the lazy ones, we'll still have five men rested and ready to raise hell."

"There is one thing you aren't considering in your little scheme."

"And what's that?"

"The rest of the town."

McFarland let loose a full-bellied laugh. "These townsfolk? Lest you forget, my dear, I own this town. I say boo, they jump. Sure, if every single person here rose against us, we'd have no choice but to move on. But that's why we spread a wide net. Every single person has something to lose by defying me... and something to gain by simply stepping back and letting me tell them what to do."

"Not every single one."

"You seem to have an overwhelming amount of faith in this sheriff. It's unbecoming, I must say."

"You talked to him. Would you say I'm mistaken?"

"I'd say any time you put your money on a man who isn't Frank McFarland, you've made a poor decision."

"Time will tell, I suppose."

"Indeed, Anne-Marie. Indeed. And perhaps it's time for a little more fun from our side. Who've we got out and about?"

"Whoever is down at the saloon, I imagine. Seems your crew never wanders too far from their barstools."

"Precisely why I picked them. Who better to cause havoc than someone who's already a few bottles in?"

The woman started to respond but instead shrugged, finished her sherry, and walked to the office door. "There is still something to be said for class. Even in this line of business."

"And yet here you stand, waist deep in it. Go rustle me up some troublemakers, Anne-Marie. And have a little faith in your boss."

The woman laughed sarcastically and walked out of the room.

***

A few days later, Chancy Rosman pushed open the batwing doors of the Horseshoe Saloon. He was tired. McFarland's new men had practically taken up a schedule for duty, causing dustups in an almost orderly fashion.

No sooner did he get one man locked up than another was bailed out. McFarland had said his pockets were deep, and Chancy was realizing it hadn't been just the bluff of an overconfident crook. It was looking like McFarland could throw enough money around to make nearly any problem go away, even if only temporarily.

Chancy had seen it before. He knew how this would play out. Eventually, one side would wear down, usually the one with the star.

And then the remaining few bandits in lockup would either be left to rot or bailed out to ride off with the rest of the crew to wherever the money was calling them next. It was a low way to live, mercenary really, taking money to disrupt folks' lives.

At least with the occasional theft, a fellow could see the need that would drive someone to it. But these men were with no motive other than disturbing the peace, ruining lives, and pushing others as far as they could, then pushing just a little farther.

Unfortunately for the gang in the Horseshoe, Chancy was tired, irritated, and just trying to get back to Teresa's for a meal and a brief rest, which meant the one thing he didn't have was much patience.

He'd assessed the situation from outside before moving in. Two of the men held one patron with his back against the bar. From where he stood, Chancy couldn't completely see what they were up to, but the way they had his arms pinned behind him and his head pulled back, it looked an awful lot like an old game called Take Him to the Well.

The game consisted only of pouring whiskey down a man's throat until he either passed out or agreed to do whatever it was the other men had requested. In Chancy's experience, the request could be anything from money to some kind of stunt, which, he recalled, was how it had all started out. Silly games between younger men adapted to the darker demands of the older.

A third man stood off to the side, hand on the butt of his gun, but more involved in watching the show than keeping an eye out for any Good Samaritans, which was likely his actual job in the matter.

Chancy scanned the room quickly, looking for unseen accomplices, checking bystanders, finding the spots that, should he need it, would provide the best cover.

From what he could see, none of the three men were familiar, and none were anywhere near sober. That meant two things: one, they'd be quick to anger, and two, they'd be poor at aiming. He scanned the room again, making eye contact with one patron nearby, and slipped between the doors.

Gesturing to the patron's table, he could spread the quiet message to sit low, be ready to hit the floor. There was no telling where a bullet could fly in a situation like this, but tipped-over tables always provided at least some cover.

He did his best to motion to the others as he moved forward quietly, fading to the side so he could approach from behind both the supposed lookout and the man holding the patron on the left. With any luck, he'd stay out of the third's sight as well.

Luck had been something in short supply of late, however, and with just a few paces left, the third man, the one he knew would be hardest to avoid, caught his movement in the mirrored glass behind the bar. Taking advantage of the momentary alcohol delay in the man's brain, Chancy leaped forward, simultaneously drawing his own gun as he deftly plucked the revolver from the lookout's holster.

Before the other two could draw, they were staring down two steady, determined barrels.

The man between them slumped to the floor, coughing and spitting up the last mouthful of whiskey.

"Having a party?" Chancy asked, moving his eyes steadily between the three, taking a step back to keep them all in a closer field of vision and, if necessary, firing position.

There was a moment of silence before one, the man on Chancy's right, finally found his voice. "If it ain't the new pet sheriff," he said, steadying himself on the bar in what failed to be a nonchalant motion.

"How about that?" Chancy said. "What're the odds, huh? Guess this fella was just having a lucky night, after all."

The man to his left smirked, glancing at the lookout. "Nice watch, Smith."

"Hey, I didn't—"

"That's enough," Chancy barked. "You boys'll have plenty of time for bickering down in the cells tonight. The only question is whether you're gonna make this easy on everybody, or do you still have a little spark left in ya? Me, I'd just as soon drop all three of you where you stand and head on to my dinner, which was where I was fixin' to be before you interrupted my plans. And I ain't any too patient when I'm hungry."

"You can't just shoot us," the lookout said. "I'm not even armed."

"You could be," Chancy flipped the man's revolver around in his hand, offering it butt-first to the startled man. "Go on, take it. You wanna play, we can play. Three-on-one odds, after all. That's what you gave this poor fella."

The men exchanged a long glance. Chancy noted the twitch of their fingers. He felt a bead of sweat roll down his back. He might take all three. It would be close, but it was a bluff he was hoping they wouldn't call. Just then, he heard bootsteps on the hardwood behind him. He glanced up at the mirror behind the bar, just in time to see a man in his mid-forties approaching the group, a small Derringer resting in the palm of his hand.

"I don't know," the man with the Derringer said. "Seems to me three on one ain't fair at all. Figure I might help even the odds." He stopped beside Chancy, the gun casually pointed between the men. "Only got two shots, but I figure after what I seen the sheriff do last month, one oughtta be plenty. You boys hear about that? So fast you can't even see his hands move. And that's when the gun ain't even out yet."

Chancy glanced over at him just as the dry click of a rifle being cocked came from his side.

A few feet down toward the end of the bar, the bartender had pulled his gun out from under the counter. "Ask me, three on three is more to my liking," the bartender said.

Chancy looked down the bar, suppressing a grin. "Well, boys. What do you say? Fair fight? Or maybe we just all call it a night?"

For a moment, the men seemed to consider it still, no doubt the alcohol tampering with their brains. Any fool could see they were too tightly packed, too far behind to have any chance of even drawing their weapons before bullets came from three different directions.

Finally, Smith slowly raised his palms. The other two looked at him, disgusted yet relieved to not have to be the first to surrender. "Ain't nothing but an overnight and you know it," Smith said.

"Overnight's long enough for me to get some food in me and meet you back out in the street tomorrow, should you feel like holding a grudge."

"May not be me," the man said, spitting at the ground, "but you give it enough time, and you will meet one of us out there. And I tell you what, friend, you ain't gonna have time to say 'damn' before you're face down in the dust."

"Then I guess I ain't got much to worry about," Chancy said. "Let's go."

Chancy lined the men up, motioning for his new friend with the Derringer to remove the remaining revolvers and toss them on the bar. "I'll be back for those after bit," Chancy said. "And much obliged, friend."

"Anytime, Sheriff."

"C'mon." Chancy gestured with the barrel of his gun toward the batwing doors. "I got some beds just waiting on you three."

The men filed out ahead of him, heads down, muttering under their breath.

Chapter 6
Jail Break

The next morning, Chancy perched on the corner of his desk. The new deputy, Ralph Whittaker, was in the chair after a long night's watch on the now-full four jail cells. All the men were part of the new crew, that much had hardly been kept secret.

Over the last few weeks, any doubt of the mass invasion had gone by the wayside. New prisoners brought in were greeted by those in the cells with guffaws, off-color jokes, and a rise in aggression toward both of the lawmen. Chancy had expected as much, but Whittaker seemed shaken.

"You can't let 'em see it," Chancy was saying in a calm, low voice. He gestured toward the keys dangling from Ralph's belt. "And the fact of the matter is, you got those and they don't. No matter what they say, not a single word is gonna make those doors spring open. So you just keep doing what you're doing. Act like you got some sense. You'll be fine."

"Makes for a long night," Ralph said, running his hands through his hair. He was in his late fifties, a man chosen for his reputation as an upstanding citizen more than for his skills as a fighter or peacemaker. Chancy wasn't sure he'd have made the same choice, but given the mayor's apparently limited options, Chancy knew he should just be thankful there was someone else to sit in for him.

After spending the first few nights at the jail desk, he knew there was no way he could keep up the fight too long. These men knew rest was coming, and they used every bit of their energy to prevent Chancy from getting any of his own. So green or not, Ralph was serving an important purpose.

"You don't have to tell me twice," Chancy said. "And I appreciate you sitting in for me. Not the most pleasant job in the world, I know, but hey, you get to just kick back. Beats digging ditches."

Ralph gave him a weak smile. "I suppose you've got a point there."

"Well, either way," Chancy said, "I'm here to relieve you, so head on home and get some rest. Way things've been going, there'll be a whole new crew in here by the time you—"

The door to the office burst open. Andy Nichols ran in with his cheeks flushed. He was out of breath. "Chancy!"

"Whoa, kid. Hey. Breathe."

The boy leaned his hands on his knees, shaking his head.

"You smell like smoke," Chancy said, walking over. "Where at?"

The boy gestured off toward the edge of town. "Our..." he gasped, "neighbor's place. The... Conroys."

"How bad?" Chancy grabbed his hat from the desk.

"Barn's going," Andy panted. "House'll be next if we don't... get help."

Chancy shot a look at Ralph, who shrugged his shoulders.

"I'll be here," the deputy said. "Get movin'."

Chancy hooked Andy by the elbow on his way by. "C'mon kid. We're gonna need every set of hands we can get."

The pair rushed back out to where Chancy's Appaloosa stood at the hitching rail. He leaped into the saddle, pulling the boy up behind him as they tore off down the main street, hollering "Fire!" to all they passed.

It would not be pretty, Chancy knew. Andy and his folks lived on the side of town that sat farthest from the lake. But the water would come. It was just a matter of how soon.

***

"All right," Marty Walker said, peering around the corner of the mercantile shop as Chancy and Andy flew off in the other direction on horseback. "Looks like now's the time."

Walker glanced back at the two men behind him. He was always the first McFarland called when things needed a fire lit under them, perhaps because he seemed to enjoy doing it so literally. Ever since they'd gotten into town, he'd been itching to drop a match somewhere.

The "juvenile stuff," as Walker called it, the fights, the rabble-rousing was child's play to him. But watching a building go up, letting nature take control of the chaos, that was something that made him feel near religious.

And now, here he was, missing out on all the fun. Sure, he'd lit the fire, but the flames were carrying on without him.

Maybe if he played his cards right, he could make it back for the tail end... but no. McFarland had explicitly told him to start the blaze and then stay away. Fool of a man at times, denying an artist the enjoyment of his work. But a fool who paid well.

He turned to the men with him: Lucas, a nine-fingered loose cannon he'd been riding with since they cut out at fifteen, and Mario, a recent addition to the crew. He didn't know the man well and, therefore, didn't like him any too much.

But they were the three chosen to hang back last night, wasting a perfectly good evening of drinking to be up and in position by sunrise.

At least they'd be done after this, and with a whole day to get good and liquored up. Maybe Marty would even find himself a lady friend, if he were feeling persuasive. That gal at the restaurant sure wasn't a bad looker.

"McFarland says there's two of 'em now," Marty said. "But that Chancy's the only one with any guts in him. New guy's just a warm body, a hand to hold the keys while the sheriff's out chasing us around. I don't reckon we'll get much of a fight out of him. So get in, get the keys, spring the boys, and head out. We'll be done in less time'n it takes me to tell you's about it."

"Then what're we talkin' for?" Lucas pulled his bandana up over his mouth, snugging the brim of his cowboy hat down low over his eyes. "In and out. Let's go."

"My thoughts exactly," Mario said, adjusting his mask as well.

"All right," Marty said. "I'll go first. Lucas, you come in behind me and go left. Mario, go right. If what McFarland said is right, the old man just sits at the desk all night, anyway. At least that's what he said the boys who've bunked there told him. And hell, ain't like he's gonna want much to do with the likes of us."

Lucas laughed from behind his bandana. "Ain't too many folks want much to do with you any day of the week."

"Can it, Luke. You can crack your jokes when there's seven of us and nobody in the cells. Follow me."

The trio slipped around the edge of the mercantile building, staying close to the wooden walls and moving swiftly through the shadows of the overhanging sidewalk roofs. The clomp of boot-heels on wood could hardly draw attention in this town. They just needed to move fast.

****

Ralph Whittaker had known it would happen eventually. He'd run through the scenario in his mind countless times since he'd accepted the deputy position.

No matter what Gerrit Travis had said, Ralph had known better. The two had gone to school and grown up together. Elkhorn was the only town they really knew. So when Travis started downplaying things, Ralph knew to expect tenfold more.

In the nights before and the days since, as he'd tried to sleep, he'd wondered how exactly he'd become "just the man for the job." Most likely, it was because of his bachelorhood. It wasn't by design, but it wasn't something he'd given much mind to. At least not until he realized it made him a rather expendable man.

Not that Travis would've used those words. But when it came down to it, even Ralph would've agreed a single man has less to lose than one with a family.

When the door to the jail burst open that day, he wondered even more what it would've been like to have one.

The three moved swiftly, unlike the men he'd seen stumbling in and out of the jail over the last few days. Perhaps, and he was baffled to even think it, but perhaps it was just that these men appeared to be sober.

He watched them spread out across the room, the movements almost practiced. If not for this incident, then one very similar to it in the past.

Shoot, he thought, this was probably just another part of the job for them. One moved off to his right, another off to his left, both staying close to the wall but spreading wide, reducing his ability to keep an eye on all three at once and increasing the odds of them having the jump on anyone unlucky enough to come through the door after them. The third, the leader Ralph had to assume, walked directly up to the desk. All three had guns drawn, but only this man had his aimed at Ralph.

"There's a real easy way to do this, old man," the gunman in front of Ralph said. "The way we figure is you ain't seen our faces, and you don't want yours blown off, so why not just hand me the keys and we'll be out of your hair?"

Ralph looked at the man, surprised at the calm he felt.

"Cat got your tongue, pardner?" the gunman moved forward. "Don't tell me you're planning on playing hero. You ain't got a snowball's chance of that. And you know as well as I do, your big burly pal just hightailed it to the other side of town. Something tells me you ain't got nothing to say so interesting it'd keep us here till he comes back. So let's go. Off with 'em. Keys on the desk."

Ralph continued to sit quietly, studying the man. If this was the day Ralph was to die, is this the man who would pull the trigger? Maybe one of the other two was more impatient. Maybe it would be an accident. An itchy finger. A stray bullet.

In the desk at his knee was an old Colt he'd had at home. Travis hadn't exactly told him to come armed, but he hadn't exactly told him not to either. As the deputy, "It's a gray area" was all Ralph had been told. Almost akin to a personal preference. Ralph was almost certain that, had the gun been visible, he wouldn't still be breathing.

He had no move. No cards to play. Even so, every second he delayed, every heartbeat was one more.

"Let's go!" the gunman barked, a lightning-quick motion bringing the barrel of the gun up the side of Ralph's head, drawing blood.

Ralph reeled, seeing stars, and jolted out of his reverie to the very real, deadly situation he found himself in. "All right, all right." He held a hand up to his temple, attempting to staunch the flow of blood before it got in his eyes, leaving him even more vulnerable than the stun of the blow already had. "There's no need for that."

"There must be some need, or I wouldn't still be standing here," Marty said. "If I have to come over there and take them keys, it's gonna be off your corpse."

Ralph nodded, drifting his free hand across his body, keeping it visible as he worked at the clasp on his belt loop, freeing the dangling ring. He tossed them onto the table. "There. Take 'em. Whatever happens, the blood's on your hands."

"Much obliged," Marty said. "And don't you be worrying about my hands. A little more blood ain't gonna hurt anything. Now, where's them fancy bracelets y'all keep around here?"

Ralph gestured toward a desk drawer, one just above where his Colt sat tucked away. If there were a time to act, it would be now.

But what were his choices, really? Slow the men down for the fraction of a second it took to put a bullet in him? Even cuffing him was more inconvenient than killing him.

"Well, get 'em then," Marty whined. "I swear, you're dumber'n a deaf mule."

Ralph leaned over and pulled the drawer open. The cuffs sat atop some papers, the keys behind them.

"Put 'em on, behind your back, and your hind end better not leave the chair, or the top of your head's going, too."

The deputy moved slowly, not out of any plan, but more out of fear of startling some unforeseen action from the outlaws. Deliberately, he removed the cuffs.

The gunman hadn't looked too closely. If Ralph could just ride it out until they were gone, the keys would still be in the back of the drawer. And below that, his piece.

"Today!" Marty raised his weapon, preparing to strike the deputy again.

"I'm moving, I'm moving," Ralph whispered. "I just didn't want you thinking I had any ideas."

"You hear that?" Marty turned to Mario. "He's finally acting smart. Look at this smart guy!"

The three men laughed as Ralph reached around behind himself, clicking the cuffs shut and leaning back in the desk chair.

"Well now, see? Ain't this just a pretty picture? You listen good, and maybe things turn out all right for ya." Marty reached down and grabbed the cell keys, tossing them across the room to Lucas. "Let's spring them boys and get."

As Lucas moved to the cells and began opening doors, Marty stepped up to the window by Mario, glancing out between the slightly parted curtains. Ralph had closed them the night before. He'd meant to open them but usually did on his way out. He looked at the sunlight streaming through.

The men filed past the desk, smirking, swearing, each with something in particular he felt he needed to say to the man who was simply asked to sit in a chair at night.

"Told ya it wouldn't take long," the last one, Smitty, Ralph thought his name was, said.

Ralph kept his eyes on the floor between his feet. He'd never asked to be a lawman. What could Travis have really expected? Three, now seven, to one? It was suicide.

"Hey!"

Ralph looked up at the voice. It was Smitty again, now standing over next to the two at the windows. "Your momma not tell you it's rude to ignore a man when he's talking to you?"

Ralph thought about replying, started to say something, though he wasn't sure what, when his mouth went dry. Smooth as can be, Smitty plucked a revolver from one man, aimed, and fired.

"What the hell'd you do that for?" Marty cuffed him up the back of the head. "You think nobody's gonna notice a damn gunshot from the sheriff's office? Let's go, boys! Move!"

The men poured out the door, scattering into the town to all the points of the compass, planning to reconvene at sundown.

As he worked his way down the wooden boardwalk, close on Marty's heels, Smitty answered, "He made us wait too long."

Chapter 7
Chancy's Eyes & Ears

Anne-Marie sauntered into Frank McFarland's office, her elegant dress a deep red and making the crisp paper of the telegram in her hand stand out in stark contrast.

"Is this what I think it is?" She waved the paper slightly in front of her.

"I don't know how you'd expect me to tell from the back, but if you mean a turn of the tide, then I likely expect so. Good news travels fast, after all."

"Yes, but bad news travels faster," she said in her breathy, deep voice.

"Well I suppose it depends on which side we fall, doesn't it? What's bad news for some might be great news for others."

The woman held his gaze and the telegram just a moment longer.

McFarland thought, as he often did, she was simply trying to see just how far she could push her limits with him. The most frustrating part was she seemed to know exactly where that line was and nimbly stepped back just before he could get angry. He raised an eyebrow, the only precursor to when he would raise his voice.

Anne-Marie let the paper fall to his desk.

McFarland grabbed it and held it close to his eyes, trying to find the sunlight for easier reading. A moment later, he smiled, the broad, greedy smile Anne-Marie had become so used to seeing over their acquaintanceship. It still made her stomach turn.

"The verdict?" she asked.

"Great, great news." McFarland grinned at her. "Great news for us, and unfortunately, terrible news for our new sheriff. Poor man barely had time to get used to the star, and now he's going to lose it."

Anne-Marie cocked her head to the side. "You planning to replace him? He seems to take to the work like a fish to water."

"Yes, yes, and I'm sad to say that is part of the problem. He has to be replaced. He must be if we plan on moving forward with our original steps. But to be replaced, well, I'm afraid this gentleman would rather die than step down from what I'm sure he sees as a noble calling."

"And so...?"

"And so," McFarland said, "we're going to introduce something new to the equation. Perhaps you've heard of Daniel Reese?"

"Perhaps I have," Anne-Marie feigned nonchalance. "The name seems to ring a bell, though I have been terribly many places in my life."

"Well, luckily for you, he is someone you'll soon be well acquainted with. Daniel Reese is someone I've had my eye on for quite some time now. Given our steady movements west, I believe you might play a bit more ignorant than you ought. His is not a name to take lightly. Unless you want to be number fifteen."

Anne-Marie raised an eyebrow.

"Yes, number fifteen. I'm hoping to reserve that number for our dear friend Chancy Rosman, but something tells me Mr. Reese doesn't have too terribly many qualms about who he meets where, just so long as he's the one who walks away. They say he's the fastest gun in this entire area, though I believe it's more like this entire state, perhaps all the surrounding ones as well. He's met fourteen men in standoffs in the last two years alone, walked away without a scratch every time. Some say the other men have died with their guns only half drawn."

"And our sheriff will be fifteen."

"I'm afraid so. Though…" McFarland leaned back in his chair. "By now, the number may have been claimed. And well, as we all know, word of mouth isn't the most reliable source of information. If I had to wager, I'd say number fifteen fell a while ago."

"Sounds like an eager employee."

"He's eager all right, but an eager businessman. You'll do well to remember that. Mr. Reese doesn't take to the idea of being in anyone's employ, per se. Partnerships, sure. But you'll want to let him do his own thing, his own way. This man isn't like our usual lot, Anne-Marie."

"You mean he won't ride in half-drunk and ride out dead?"

"Yes, well, as we know, one often gets what one pays for. But given our previous circumstances, we could skimp a little on our tools, shall we say? A new situation requires a fresh approach, even if the plan is not entirely reevaluated."

"I'm sure I cannot see how this man is any different from the rest of your hired guns. Maybe faster, but as we saw not so long ago, faster is a rather relative term."

"Which is why I wanted the fastest. Mark my words, Anne-Marie, Daniel Reese is going to solve this problem for us. And if I had to wager, I'd imagine he'll collect his fee and disappear afterward."

"You aren't usually one for a single job."

"And I'm hoping, after all this, Mr. Reese won't be either."

"So when can we expect this new miracle man?"

"Within twenty-four hours. And I'd say, within forty-eight hours after that, we should be back to business as usual."

Anne-Marie looked at the man with half-closed eyes. "I suppose we shall see."

"Indeed we shall."

***

The next day, Chancy was leaning on the counter of the mercantile shop, taking a few blessed moments away from riding up and down the streets, interrupting bar brawls and chasing down the new breed of local nuisance.

"I'm glad to hear everything turned out all right," he was saying to Andy.

"For the neighbors at least," Andy said. "But, I... well..."

"Look, kid, Ralph knew what he was getting into. Maybe he didn't think it would get so hot so fast, but that's always something you gotta consider when you sit behind that desk. Hanging our heads about it ain't gonna bring in those men any faster. We gotta stay alert, keep our eyes open. Every person in this town, whether they live here or are just passing through, makes at least one stop. And that's to you. You be smart and pay attention. We'll figure out who did this to Ralph, and I'll make sure they swing for it."

The boy cringed a little.

"I know, it's not a pretty idea, but neither is shooting a man down like they did. They treated him like a dog. Far as I'm concerned, they made the rules right then."

"I just wish I hadn't've come for you," Andy said, looking down.

"You did the right thing," Chancy said. "It's what I'd have done in your shoes."

The boy looked up a little at this, the compliment carrying all the weight Chancy had hoped it would. "So you aren't mad?"

"Oh, I'm plenty mad," Chancy said. "Just not at you. What'm I to be mad at you for? Thanks to you, the Conroys still got their house. You keep thinking quick and trusting your gut, and you'll be just fine."

"Well, about that," Andy started, then trailed off again.

"What is it?"

"Ah, it's just rumors. I can't imagine there'd be any truth to 'em."

"But there might be. Like I said, kid, you're the one with the information. You're the one who hears things. You may not like being treated like a servant or a youth in here, but I'll tell you something right now. That's your biggest weapon. When people think nobody's listening, they'll say a whole lotta things. Maybe they are just spreading gossip. You and me both know Elkhorn's got more'n its share of blowhards."

Andy laughed.

"But you aren't ever gonna be doing wrong to tell me what you heard. If it don't pan out, we ain't lost nothing. If it does, though, well, you'd be doing me a real favor."

The boy smiled again, proud not only to be treated like an adult but like something almost akin to a partner by this no-nonsense man. "All right, well, here's the thing." Andy leaned on the counter, unconsciously mimicking Chancy's posture. "You ever hear the name Daniel Reese?"

Chancy looked up, running through his memory. "Believe I may've. Remind me."

"Like I said, all this is just hearsay, but the general knowledge is he's the fastest draw out this way. According to some, he has killed ten men in the last couple years. Some say a dozen. Some say more. But however many it is, you can just about bet one thing, and that's that he's been killing and word's been traveling."

"And does word say he's heading in our direction?" Chancy asked.

"Word says he's fixing to be here tonight, if he ain't already."

Chancy rubbed at the back of his neck. "Well, that is certainly some news, ain't it?"

"If it's true, I'd say so. If it ain't, well…"

"If it ain't, that's just fine by me. I appreciate you letting me know if it is. Sounds like the kind of fella I oughtta be keeping an eye on."

"Just…" Andy looked at his hands again. "Just be careful doing it. If the stories are even half-true, this cowboy is one who really likes to find reasons to draw down."

"And you're thinking he's here to find a reason with me?"

Andy shrugged. "Can you think of any other reason? You've made more than a few people mad around here.. I know me and my folks are more than thankful you stepped up when you did, but…"

"But sometimes it takes a little more to solve the problem. I get ya." Chancy straightened up and extended a hand. "Andy, you're making a fine man of yourself here, and I'm much obliged to ya."

Andy reached out, shaking the man's rough hand.

"You keep your eyes and ears open. I gotta go mosey about and see what kind of trash I can kick up. But I'll be checking in with you periodically. Something comes up you think I need to know, you come find me. If you can't find me, I'll tell Mrs. Slayton to keep an eye out for you."

The boy blushed a little.

"That all right?" Chancy asked.

"Yeah, yeah," Andy looked at the man, then quickly added. "It's not like that. I mean, Mrs. Slayton's a fine woman. Her daughter as well. I just… well…"

Chancy leaned over and patted the boy on the shoulder. "You're doing fine work. You oughtta be treated so, partner."

The boy smiled wider, turning even redder.

"Keep it up, kid."

"Yes, sir."

Chancy adjusted his hat, sighed almost imperceptibly at the door, then walked back out into the bright Nebraska sun.

***

That evening, Frank McFarland sat in the bunkhouse of his ranch, a place he seldom visited, not at all if he could manage it. However, the man across the rough-hewn table from him had had a long ride and, if McFarland was reading him right, felt more comfortable on a wooden chair than a plush velvet one.

McFarland had attempted some version of small talk, but Daniel Reese was a man of few words, grunts mostly, when the topic strayed to anything that could be considered even slightly trivial.

"You're offering a pretty penny for this feller's hide," Reese said, one arm slung over the back of his chair. "Ordinarily, that'd make me think you was bluffing me."

"I can assure you, that would be the last thing I would do," McFarland said.

"Yeah, you and everybody else. I did some askin' though, and the general consensus is you's on the up and up. At least so long as I don't get my own damn head blowed off. Folks who come around you don't seem to last too long."

"I expect quality work, and unfortunately, as you I'm sure know, it is often difficult to find quality men."

Reese moved a toothpick from one side of his mouth to the other.

"I'll be quite honest with you," McFarland continued after a silence. "This Rosman fellow is no slouch. I've seen him in a standoff, and well, he's fast. Very fast." Before McFarland could blink, he was staring down the barrel of one of Reese's revolvers.

"That fast?" the gunslinger asked.

McFarland licked his lips. For a man who so easily invoked violence in his daily affairs, he preferred it at a much greater distance. "I highly doubt it."

"You 'highly doubt it,'" Reese mocked. "Well, you do that. Because I know he ain't. Ain't no man that fast, asides me. I'd tell you to ask around, but ain't too many people who seen that still breathing to tell you so."

"I'm sure you're quite right," McFarland said. "Now, if you could…" He gestured toward the gun.

Reese hesitated for a moment, clearly enjoying the man's discomfort, then slowly uncocked the revolver and slid it back into its holster.

"So how you wantin' it done?" Reese asked. "I ain't much for shooting a man in his back, but truth be told, I ain't much for rules, either."

"Yes," McFarland said. "Well, you see, this is somewhat of a delicate matter, given he is the sheriff here."

Reese raised an eyebrow.

"Well, temporarily," McFarland added hastily. "Our previous lawman had a bit of an incident with a man who, as I'm sure you're familiar, was faster. Now everything had been running along smoothly up till that point. But then our mayor had this brilliant scheme to mess around in affairs he had no business messing around in, and, well…" He shrugged.

"And somebody needs to remind him of his place."

McFarland smiled. "That's a nice way to put it."

"Tell you what." Reese grinned. "You sweeten the pot a little, and I could take care of both of 'em while I'm here. Wouldn't take no time at all."

McFarland leaned back in his chair, folding his arms. "I certainly do like the way you think," he said. "But I believe our mayor might yet still serve some purpose, so long as he gets his mind back where it belongs. You pose an interesting idea, though. I may take you up on that someday."

"Well, someday I may not be so interested."

"Quite right," McFarland said. "But for now, let's simply focus on the matter at hand. Sheriff Rosman."

Reese spat the toothpick to the floor, waving his hand in a "carry on" gesture.

"Given that he is, even temporarily, the recognized law in this town, I'll need you to have at least some finesse in this. Draw him out. Egg him on. Anything that gets you in a position of self-defense rather than aggression."

"Seems a little overly complicated for putting a bullet in a man."

"Perhaps, but we like things clean here. *I* like things clean. And as you said, I may need to buy your services at a later date. It wouldn't do to have to spring you from some calaboose in order to do so."

"All right, so get him to draw on me. Won't be the first time that occurred."

"I imagine not."

Reese looked at McFarland, seeming almost unsure whether he wanted to remind the businessman of how fast his hand was again.

"The point being," McFarland hurried on, "you have proven yourself adept at coming out of those situations alive. And that's what I require. One sheriff problem solved by a man who knows how to do it."

"And all for a grand," Reese said.

"One thousand dollars, yes."

"I'd say you got yourself a gun then."

"Excellent." McFarland grinned broadly. "Now, what exactly can I be expecting for this fee?"

"Besides a dead sheriff?" Reese smiled.

"I was thinking more of some idea of how you plan to go about this."

"You just stay cool, cowpoke," Reese said. "Give me a day or two to get a feel for this place. Was a long ride out here, after all. Gotta let a feller get settled in, or I'm gonna get my feelings hurt."

McFarland stared at the man for a moment, then chuckled. "Take all the time you need. What's mine is yours, and that includes—should this go well—the entire town."

"Now, see, I like the sound of that," Reese said.

"Simply keep me posted, then." McFarland stood, catching a glare from the man. "I simply request it as a courtesy, not an order."

Reese nodded and shooed the man out of the bunkhouse.

Chapter 8
Plans Gone Awry

That night, Chancy stretched his legs up on the front porch railing alongside Teresa, a full meal in his belly. Betsy went off to bed, and a few moments of blessed silence hovered over the town.

It wouldn't last. He knew better than to hope for that. But for just these few minutes, while the lawlessness itself even seemed to need a break, he was content to rest his weary body.

Teresa rocked in a chair beside him, looking out into the night, thinking her own thoughts but apparently content to keep them to herself, simply being thankful the man she thought of as her friend was back home again, safe.

A cool breeze blew through the nighttime air, carrying only a few soft sounds from the town toward them. Out on the edge like they were, they could hear the occasional coyote howling with his pack, bringing an eerie though somehow calming tone to the quiet of the porch.

"I talked to Andy today," Chancy finally said, turning his head slightly to see the woman.

"You've taken a shine to him."

Chancy laughed. "He's a good kid. Got a future if we can keep him moving forward."

"That shouldn't be too hard."

"Shouldn't be, but nothing out here ever seems too easy, either."

"Nonsense. That boy would swim the Missouri for you if you asked him."

"Side to side?" Chancy grinned.

"Down to the gulf, I imagine. He's taken quite the shine to you as well, as I'm sure you've noticed."

"Ah." Chancy adjusted his feet on the rail. "He's got a solid head on his shoulders. He oughtta know better than to be following in the footsteps of somebody like me."

"Maybe."

Chancy looked over at Teresa, catching a slight grin. "But better me than half the folks in this town."

"Oh, is that a fact?"

"Which side are you taking here?" he laughed.

"Whichever one you aren't, naturally. Someone's got to keep you in line."

"I don't envy that, woman."

"Nor do I," Teresa laughed with him.

"He may come up this way from time to time," Chancy said. "Thought I should let you know."

"Oh, Chancy." Teresa folded her hands in her lap. "Don't go getting that boy involved in your troubles."

"I'm not, I'm not." He pressed the air with open palms. "At least not in any way that he isn't already."

"What's that supposed to mean?"

"Just that he stands in that shop all day long, and he's got working ears and eyes."

"Sometimes even that's all it takes."

"And that's why I told him to keep you in mind. People see him running up to me every whipstitch or, even worse, into the sheriff's office, they'll cotton on to him quicker'n you can spit. But out here, well, he's already making deliveries regular enough. There's always something we can use. If some information comes along with the cornmeal, nobody can help that, now, can they?"

"And then I'm to run and fetch you? What makes you think I want to be the one seen chasing after you all day long? Besides, I've got more than plenty to keep myself and Betsy occupied here. Thank you kindly."

"No, no," Chancy sighed. "You just keep doing what you're doing. You don't change a thing."

"And if some information comes along with your cornbread?"

"You do make a darn good cornbread."

"Flattery will get you everywhere," Teresa laughed.

Chancy sighed.

"What is it?"

"I'm just ready for this to be done."

"I thought you liked being the sheriff."

"I liked the idea," Chancy mused. "I didn't realize this town was going to lose its marbles as soon as I pinned on the star."

"Ah."

The pair sat in silence for a moment, Chancy thinking his thoughts and Teresa waiting for him to share them.

"You've been here a good while now," he said. "You've seen things. I don't suppose they're just testing the new sheriff out, are they?"

The woman laughed again. "If they are, this is one test I've never seen before. I haven't set foot in town proper since your second day, and until whatever is going on gets settled, I don't have any plans to. We do just fine out here on our own, and I have no desire to change that."

"Yeah," Chancy said. "Yeah, I was kinda thinking that same thing. I suppose there's only one thing to do about it then."

"Are you sure that's best?" It was one thing Chancy respected and appreciate most about the woman. She was sharp. He'd never doubted that. But her ability to see through his eyes, to cut to the heart of a problem without wishful thinking getting in the way, was something he'd always admired in another man or woman.

"I reckon I can either keep plugging holes in the levee or get to the source of the problem. I don't know about you, but I'm getting pretty near wore out by hole plugging."

"Just make sure you don't come back with more holes than you leave with."

"That is perhaps the one thing I ain't concerned about. Leastwise, not tomorrow."

"No?"

"Nah," he said. "The way I figure, McFarland isn't too eager to get his hands dirty 'less it's off a dusty greenback. And even then, I imagine he'd get somebody to hand him gloves first. No, I go out there and talk to the man, meet him on his own ground. It might rattle him, sure, but that's one thing I'm okay with. What I don't like is him sitting in the background, pulling all the strings and going about his day with the whole town, pretending they don't know he's doing it."

"It still seems risky. What if there are others out there? Many men would be happy to put a bullet in you if Frank gives the nod."

"That is very true," Chancy said, settling his feet on the ground. He leaned his elbows on his knees and looked over at Teresa. "What we're gonna have to hope is old Frank won't be too keen on it happening on his own property. Something like that just opens the door for all kinds of folks to poke around. I suppose right now the smart move is to just sit down and see what he's got to say."

"And then?"

"Yes," he nodded. "That's the part I'm trying to figure out as well. Ain't no use trying to pull the wool over your eyes, I know that. So what I'm wondering is what happens when Frank McFarland gets his cage rattled. I reckon I'll be safe while I'm out there, but once the horse hooves cross the property line, well…"

Teresa leaned forward, trying to catch his eye with hers. "There are other ways. You could put in a call for more men, for instance. Talk to the mayor."

"Yeah, I thought about that. Seems to me, if the mayor was gonna squash this bug, he'd have dirty boots already. I know you vouch for the man, but I don't know how far I'd trust him yet."

"You think he's in McFarland's pocket, too?"

"Not necessarily. Mayhap he's just doing the best he can with what he's got. Too nervous to fight, too scared to tuck tail. I think old Travis is just sitting in his room every night, praying this thing will take care of itself."

"And you're the one to answer that prayer?"

"Teresa, I wish I knew. I surely do." Chancy stood up and stretched, his back cracking. "All I know right now is that I need some rest before I'm going to be able to do anything tomorrow. Them boys're about to run me ragged."

Teresa stood and moved to the door. "Get some rest, Chancy. The town will still be here in the morning. Or at least I imagine so."

Chancy grinned at the dark humor. "As long as I'm breathing, this house will be, leastwise. I can promise you that."

"Oh? And what good is a boarding house with no boarders?"

"Hey, you got one."

Teresa rolled her eyes. "So do your best to keep it that way."

Chancy smiled. "Yes, ma'am."

***

The next morning, Chancy rose early, wanting to get out to the McFarland ranch before the man left for town, but even more wanting to get there while McFarland's men were still hungover or sleeping the night off.

Knowing that some of them bunked and camped on the businessman's property did nothing to settle Chancy's nerves. But he hoped a visit that ended in no arrests might ease the tension somewhat.

As much as he hated to leave empty-handed, he knew he had to play it cool, at least once, to give the man a chance. A snowball's chance, maybe, but at least he could say he tried before things got worse.

Chancy rode at a leisurely pace, wanting to both give off an attitude of indifference and to make his presence known well before he crossed onto the man's property. McFarland might seem predictable in some ways, but "might" didn't do a fellow much good with a bullet in his gut.

He surveyed the land on his approach. It wasn't anything special on the surface, not until one took in the sheer size of the property.

He'd known McFarland would set up base in the most imposing way possible. Men like him always did. It was yet another way to send a message saying nothing.

And Chancy had to give him credit, the sprawling acres, the fenceposts disappearing off in the distance, the outbuildings, stables, bunkhouse… The very number of structures on the land made it that the man who lived here was not someone to be trifled with.

Unfortunately, trifling was basically Chancy's very intention.

He rode the Appaloosa at a walk through the main gate, keeping his eyes searching near and far, side to side, but not a soul seemed to be up and about. A trickle of smoke came from the chimney of what Chancy assumed was the main house, so he directed his animal that way.

Not more than halfway down the drive, though, a blur from the left caught his eye.

Chancy turned when, simultaneously from his right and straight ahead, two more forms rushed out toward him.

The sounds were guttural, deep, menacing.

The horse reared up under him, eyes wide in her sockets, as from all four points of the compass, sleek, broad-shouldered guard dogs raced up around him.

The animals stopped just short of the horse's flailing hooves, prancing back and forth as they nipped and snapped from a safe distance. Their haunches were in the air, forelimbs low and splayed. Chancy knew one step out of the stirrups would get him a jaw locked on his leg.

He patted at the horse, settling her as best he could while the dogs jumped back and forth, darting in and out, doing everything they could to keep the animal in a frenzy of fear.

"Go on, now!" Chancy hollered down, knowing it was likely to only increase the dogs' behavior but having no other option. If they kept it up, one was sure to have a hoof come down on its head. "Get!"

Chancy took off his hat, waving it at the dogs, trying to split his time between soothing the animal beneath him while still showing dominance over the ones at her legs.

A shrill whistle cut through the growls and snaps, drawing the dogs' attention, if not their bodies, away momentarily.

Chancy settled the horse beneath him before anything else, patting her neck and whispering into her ear. It was all nonsense, and truth be told, he didn't want to be there any more than the horse did, but they had work to do, and as the animal was his only partner in it, they needed to be working in sync.

The Appaloosa finally returned to all four feet on the ground, though Chancy could feel the tension in her muscles, the twitching in her haunches and back as she kept a wary eye on the dogs, whipping her large head from side to side whenever she picked up the slightest movement.

To their credit, the movements were only of the slightest nature. A paw digging into the earth. A string of drool dripping from a powerful jaw. The dogs wanted blood, but something in their nature or their training kept them in place.

"Perhaps you see why I don't encourage unannounced visitors," Frank McFarland said, walking up to the ring of dogs, taking a position next to the one ahead of Chancy, slightly to the right. "A man could find himself in a real world of hurt trespassing out here."

"That what you're planning on saying this was?"

McFarland laughed. "Come now, Rosman, you're the sheriff. Surely you have the lawful right to go anywhere you please."

"Assuming I don't mind having a chunk bit outta my leg." He reached down and patted the horse, who seemed to find no more comfort in McFarland's presence than Chancy did.

"It's the way of the west," McFarland said. "Surely you know that. A town can have lawmen like yourself, but at the end of the day, a man's got to look out for his own."

"You're certainly doing a job of that." Chancy glanced off to the side, not detecting any movement in the dogs but not entirely trusting McFarland's line of thinking. "You wanna send them boys back up to the house? Me and you can have a little chat?"

McFarland looked at the dogs on either side of him. "No," he finally said. "No, I don't think I will. After all, I really have no idea why you're here. A man can't be too careful in these instances."

Chancy glanced around himself again. The dogs maintained their distance, but he could see they were already getting restless, reaching the end of their trained patience. He let his hand fall to the butt of his revolver. "That really goes for both sides here."

McFarland laughed. "Surely you can't be serious. You mean to tell me you would come out here, unannounced no less, and shoot one of these poor animals? One who is merely doing his job? His lawfully acknowledged job?"

"Not sure I'd stop with just one," Chancy muttered.

"Oh, don't be childish," McFarland said. "It's an unbecoming trait in a man when he can't see he is in a weaker position."

"That a fact?"

"Do you feel proud of yourself now? You came out here—for what, I can't imagine—and have been bested before you even made it to my door. And not by cunning guards, but by brutes. By animals. And yet the mayor trusts you above anyone else to keep us safe. No, I don't think I'd be holding my head too high if I were the one in the saddle right now."

"Look," Chancy said between gritted teeth. "I didn't come out here to arrest nobody. I came out here just to talk. As a courtesy."

"Oh, a courtesy? Well, how very respectable of you. Though I must say, common courtesy would be to visit a man in his place of business, when wanting to talk business, not arrive suddenly in the middle of his morning meal."

"Yeah, well, let's just say I wanted to go above and beyond for a fella such as yourself."

"You flatter me," McFarland laughed.

Chancy felt his fingers tighten around the butt of his gun then, noticing McFarland eying his hand, forced himself to loosen his grip, moving the hand to the pommel instead. "I'm just asking for a few minutes of your time. Man to man."

"Yes." McFarland stroked his chin. "I see that. And while I can't say I don't enjoy the ridiculous way you're going about that, I'm afraid I'm going to have to deny your request." He turned his back on the sheriff and started back toward the house.

"I'm trying to be civil here, Frank. This may be your only chance."

The man stopped and slowly turned back to face Chancy. "Civil? Is that it? So my options are either this, or you gun me down in the street like you did to poor Lennie Aldridge?"

"Poor Lennie, my foot," Chancy snorted. "Only thing to pity in that man is he really believed he was fast."

"Ah yes," McFarland said. "That does seem to be the scourge of the west. Pride. Hubris. Every man believing he is truly the best, the fastest, the strongest, so on and so on, when as we both know, there will always be someone better."

Chancy eyed him. "I don't think much of your philosophizing. I'm just a country sheriff and all. Why don't you come out and say what it is you're wanting me to hear, Frank?"

"I prefer, Mr. McFarland, if you don't mind." Making a small motion with his hand, the four dogs came to stand at attention, two on either side of him. "Or, actually, even if you mind. Now I believe our business here has concluded."

"See, now, I don't think it has," Chancy said, glaring at the man.

McFarland nodded once, curt. "I suppose you have until I'm back inside to change your mind, then. The dogs will listen while I'm here, but I can't say what might happen once my back is turned."

"You can't go siccing your dogs on me, and you know it."

"Quite right," McFarland said. "But, as I mentioned, you are an uninvited guest, and I am well within my rights to protect my person and my property. I do so with these dogs. I know you could shoot them, probably pick off all four before they got too close for comfort, but is that something you'd like to spend your day discussing with a judge? Or something you'd want the lovely townsfolk to hear? That their sheriff is so cold-blooded and inept, he has to kill a man's dogs just to have a conversation? I suppose the choice is up to you, but, well..." McFarland trailed off, turning on his heel and slowly wandering back up toward the ranch house.

"We aren't done yet!" Chancy hollered after him.

"Oh, but for now, we certainly are," McFarland called back over his shoulder.

Chancy looked at the dogs following their master, obediently if not entirely willingly. The horse shook her mane, rolling her neck around, anxious. "All right, all right," Chancy said under his breath to the animal. "Let's go come up with a new plan."

He reined the animal around and set off at a trot back toward his office downtown.

Chapter 9
The New Hired Gun

Chancy's visit to the McFarland ranch not only didn't turn out the way he'd hoped, it seemed to only fan the flames of lawlessness in Elkhorn.

He'd known there was a risk in poking the sleeping bear, but then again, he'd thought McFarland hadn't been playing things low-key since Chancy had pinned on the star.

If he could just pin Ralph's murder on McFarland as easily.

In the forty-eight hours since he'd met McFarland's guard dogs, however, McFarland's hell-raisers had been back at it in full force.

The jail had become nothing more than a revolving door for the roughnecks, and while the town was bringing in a new wave of money through bail, Chancy was struggling to keep up with the back-and-forth trips to the cells.

At one point, he organized his papers based on who would get out soonest to not waste his time being too far away from the jail. And he never liked to make a trip back empty-handed.

Perhaps the only good thing in it all was the men seemed under orders to not resist, or at least not too strongly. It seemed McFarland's plan was to simply slowly peck away at the sheriff until there was nothing left.

At least that's how Chancy was feeling.

He'd slept only four solid hours in the last two days, sneaking in brief naps when and where he could.

If there was just a time of day when everyone settled down, he thought. But as before, the trouble came in waves. Whether it was morning, noon, or night, Chancy had to put in little legwork to find a brawl somewhere in the town.

He was riding slowly down the main street, intending to stop in at the mercantile and pick up a few things for Teresa, when it dawned on him.

In spite of the reckless and nearly constant lawless actions of the select new members of the town, he'd ridden in from the eastern edge of town with no one waving him down, without hearing the breaking glass and wood of a bar fight, without the sound of gunfire.

He could actually hear the Appaloosa's hooves on the hard-packed dirt beneath him. And the silence made him more uncomfortable than any amount of violence had so far.

He always checked side to side when he rode through town like this. The many storefronts and alleys gave too many opportunities to hide in the shadows. But now he began checking behind him as well.

He supposed to some it looked cowardly, less than sure of himself, but Chancy hadn't ever been much for appearances. And he certainly wouldn't look good with a bullet in his back, anyway.

As he hitched his horse in front of the mercantile, he glanced around him again. Nothing but wind and dust. That was when the low but stern voice from inside the store caught his ear. This wasn't like the others he'd become used to.

Most crimes in the last few days had been blatant, created purely for his attention. Given the deadness of the town, however, Chancy had to wonder at just what exactly he was walking into.

It stood to reason that, if something big were going down, a slew of distracting circumstances would've been an easy way to keep him occupied. Then again, the more elements involved in a plan, the more likely one was to go awry.

He slipped up to the front wall of the building, inching his way along the wooden boardwalk and up to the window.

He removed his hat and leaned slightly forward, glimpsing the inside through the open curtains. Andy stood, as always, behind the counter. Nothing out of the ordinary there.

What Chancy didn't like was the look on Andy's face. There was pure fear in the boy's eyes. Across from Andy stood a tall, dark-dressed man, one Chancy didn't recognize, though that hardly meant much over the last few weeks.

All Chancy was concerned about was the long-barreled revolver the man had pointed at Andy's head.

Chancy could catch the tones of the conversation if not the words. Andy's voice was higher, shakier, pleading. The man was gruff, low, and direct.

Chancy reached down and pulled his gun from the holster, checking the chambers out of habit. Only in the few moments after firing was he ever not fully loaded these days.

He chewed on his options momentarily. He could burst inside, taking the man by surprise, but if the fellow had even the slightest twitch in his trigger finger, that could be the end of things for Andy.

He could try to draw the man out, but that left Chancy exposed to too many angles, hiding places, and potential unseen accomplices. No, as much as he hated to do it, there was only one way to handle a situation like this.

Chancy holstered his weapon, set his hat firmly back on his head, and walked straight through the front door.

Immediately, the man whirled around. Chancy'd kept his hands away from his body as he entered, hoping the man would be quick enough to notice they were empty before making a rash decision.

Empty, yes, Chancy thought, but certainly not up. He kept his hands out to his sides, for all intents and purposes showing a sign of goodwill but, in reality, keeping them just a few feet closer to his revolvers.

The man eyed him momentarily as Chancy stood a few feet inside the front door.

A bandana was pulled up over the man's mouth and nose, something else that gave Chancy pause. Most of the men he'd dealt with so far had felt no qualms about showing their faces before, during, and after the crime.

This could mean one of two things: either the man holding up the mercantile was completely uninvolved with McFarland, which seemed unlikely given the man's stranglehold on the town, or this was someone who McFarland wasn't quite ready for Chancy to meet yet.

"Well, well, I was wonderin' when you'd finally make your appearance," the man said. His voice was low but clear, calm in an unnerving way.

Chancy wanted to breathe a sigh of relief, hoping the scene before him was just bluster and show, yet another attempt to draw him out. Though he couldn't help but wonder, if the man had wanted his attention, why hadn't he made a bigger commotion to begin with?

"I was just making the acquaintance of your partner here," the man said, gesturing toward Andy with the barrel of the gun. "It's clever of you. I'll give ya that. If anybody in this town's gonna see everything that shakes out, it's the feller at the mercantile."

He drew the final syllable out, pronouncing it like the color teal. He certainly wasn't from these parts, Chancy noted.

"Problem with that is," the man continued, "it seems a little sneaky, ya ask me. I figured you for a feller who'd play on the up and up. Fight his own fights, track his own men down. Not somebody who'd pull in some ragtag boy to do half his work for him. Oh, wait," the man laughed. "You did used to have yourself a deputy, didn't ya? Though I heard that ol' boy wasn't worth the chair he was sitting in when he caught that bullet."

"You seem to know an awful lot about what's going on here," Chancy said, attempting to keep the man's attention on himself. "Puts me at a disadvantage, though. I don't reckon I've seen you around these parts before. But with your little mask there, it's hard to say. Whatcha hiding under there, friend? You got one of them mugs that'll scare the horses off?"

The man laughed. "There's no need for unpleasantness. You insult every new feller that comes into your town?"

"Only the ones cowardly enough to draw on an unarmed kid."

The man laughed again, louder, and turned back to Andy. "Come on, boy. Show him what you were attempting to show me." He gestured with the barrel of the gun again.

Andy looked over at Chancy, a mixture of pleading and apology in his eyes.

"Go ahead," Chancy said. "Everything's under control."

"Ain't that sweet?" the man chuckled. "But you heard him, boy. Go on now."

Slowly, Andy reached under the counter and pulled out an ancient-looking shotgun. Even from where Chancy stood, he could see the rust marks pocked up and down along the barrel. Poor kid would be as likely to have the thing blow up in his hands as he would be to hit any target with it. Assuming he even knew how to work the machine.

"Now don't that strike you as something, Sheriff?" the man taunted. "Feller comes in here, minding his own business, and some street rat pulls out a damn blunderbuss on him. Now I'm new in town, I'll give you that, but that is one hell of a welcoming committee ya got right there." He turned to Andy. "Go on, kid. Show him how you showed me. Show him how you welcome folks into your business here."

"Andy..." Chancy pressed at the air with his open palms. "Stay calm. We all know you didn't mean nothing by it. Just a little agitated by all the goings-on here lately. Just set that gun there on the counter."

"You'll do no such thing," the man barked, his voice clear, crisp. "I tol' you, show the sheriff how you welcome folks into this here business."

Andy's hands shook, the shotgun wavering in his hands.

"Come on! Do it!" the man yelled.

"I get the point," Chancy said, trying to distract the outlaw. "Nobody wants to be surprised like that. I get it, I get it. But hey, you were looking for me, not him. And you found me. So let the kid be."

"Let the kid be?" the man laughed. "Let him be? That's how you're running things here? Well, it ain't no wonder this town's gone to hell in a handbasket then. Every yahoo pulling out guns from here, there, and everywhere. Sounds a mite lawless, if you ask me."

"You're right," Chancy said. "Andy didn't have no business with that gun. And if you'll let me do my job, I'll make sure it doesn't happen again."

"Hm," the man mused, scratching at his chin under the handkerchief with the barrel of his revolver for a moment. "That is an option." He looked between the man and the boy. "But I gotta say, you haven't exactly instilled much faith in your sheriffin' so far. Seems to me, out here in this ol' wild west, a man's gotta take care of his own problems if he wants to keep waking up every day." He turned back to Andy.

"Now seeing as how you pulled that gun out on me first, I suppose I oughtta just shoot you where you stand and be done with it. But..." He glanced at the sheriff. "That don't seem real fair now, does it? After all, the moment passed. Now, I'd just be a feller shooting a tot. Don't seem quite right, do it?"

"I ain't here to worry about who did what first," Chancy said. "I'm just here to settle things back down. How's about you holster that revolver, Andy'll drop that gun—which it looks like he'd be more than happy to do already—and we'll just get on with our day. No harm done."

"That is an option," the man said.

As Chancy watched, the gunslinger lowered his weapon. He held it about waist-high, looking at the gleam in the well-oiled steel, weighing it in his hand almost as if he could feel the dead souls it had created. He spun the gun on his finger once, twice, and slipped it back into the holster.

Chancy allowed himself a deep breath as the man walked over toward him. "Lower that, Andy. You're all right."

The man walked up and put his hand on Chancy's shoulders. The sheriff could see the smile in the man's eyes, even with the lower half of his face covered.

"So that's how you handle things here, is it, Sheriff? Everybody just makes nice, and we go on about our day, assuming ain't nothing bad gonna happen, cause if it do, you'll be there to make everybody play nice. That's an interesting way of looking at things."

Over the man's shoulder, Chancy could see Andy hesitating with the shotgun. *Put it down*, he thought at the kid. *Put that thing on the counter and step back.*

Instead, Andy's grip firmed on the barrel of the gun. Chancy gestured slightly, low, willing the kid to use his brain. There was no way Andy could shoot the man without hitting them both—the boy had to know that. And this was no time for bluster.

The gunslinger looked into Chancy's eyes, registering something, and laughed.

"See? Now right there's your problem. You can mosey around with your shiny star and your fancy uniform, but the fact is the only power you got is the power we decide to give you."

Chancy watched as Andy raised the gun to his shoulder, pleading desperately for the boy to act like a boy again, to not choose this moment to take a stand.

"But the fact is," the man said softly, "I don't reckon too many folks around here feel like giving away much of anything."

"Get out of my store," Andy said, his cheek pressed against the handle of the gun. "You ain't welcome, and the sheriff wants you to leave."

The man laughed again, his same irritating cocky laugh. "I guess now you see how little power you actually got. Can't even keep a boy in line."

"Andy…" Chancy said.

"Maybe I'll give you a little lesson in that."

The man was fast. Faster than Chancy would've believed if he hadn't been standing there to witness it. The movements were a blur.

Before he could act, the man had spun, drawn, and fired once, spinning Andy around.

The gun clattered to the counter and then to the floor, hitting the wooden planks just moments after Andy's body.

Chancy reached for the man's arm but was already too slow. The gunslinger had taken a step back in the firing motion and now the barrel rested calmly between Chancy's eyes.

"Seems to me that was pure self-defense," the man laughed. "So I'll tell you what. Consider this the one favor you'll ever get out of me."

"Shooting a child?" Chancy gritted his teeth. Every muscle in his body was tense, begging for action.

"Aw, hell," the man said. "He ain't dead. If I'd've wanted that, we'd be wiping brain splatters off ourselves right now. This here, though, this is your warning. Next time, me and you cross paths, or me and any of your little wannabe lawmen, I won't aim so kindly."

Chancy stared at the man who slogged his way toward the door, the barrel of the gun never wavering from its deadly aim.

"I reckon you oughtta go find yourself a good sawbones," the man said as he reached behind himself to open the door. "He ain't dead yet, but the clock's sure ticking a little faster than it was a moment ago."

Chancy watched as the man slipped outside, then raced over to the counter. Andy lay in a growing pool of blood behind the counter, a ragged red hole in the left shoulder of his shirt.

The man hadn't lied. And the worse part was, it had been one hell of a shot. And fast. So fast.

Chancy kicked the gun away and boosted the unconscious boy up over his shoulder, working his way back around the counter and to the door. The concern he felt in his chest, the desperate need to hurry and get the boy to the doctor, was almost overshadowed by the dark, cold anger in the lawman's eyes.

***

"You did what, now, exactly?" Frank McFarland said.

The businessman paced back and forth behind the desk in his office. Anne-Marie sat, poised as ever, in one of the plush chairs across from him. Daniel Reese stood in the center of the room, his handkerchief down around his neck now, a toothpick back in the corner of his mouth.

"You said we needed to give him a reason, so I gave him one."

"By killing a child? Are you crazy?"

"Aw, I didn't kill nobody," Reese said. "I just gave him a little lesson. He oughtta thank me for it. Got a story to tell now. The only man Daniel Reese ever shot who lived to tell the tale."

"Calling him a man seems a bit of a stretch." McFarland ran his hands through his hair. "What is he, eleven? Twelve?"

Reese shrugged. "He's old enough to pull a gun on me. He's old enough to deal with the consequences."

"And the sheriff?"

Reese smiled. "I reckon he's at the doctor's with the boy now. Probably sniveling over what a poor job he done of protecting the innocent and all that."

"I fear you may have underestimated this man if you even slightly consider him capable of sniveling."

"I surely hope I have," Reese said. "Because if the man I saw today is the one you're paying a thousand bucks to be rid of, it surely don't say much for the posse you got running with you right now."

McFarland looked at Anne-Marie, who was barely trying to suppress a smile behind her hand.

"Well," McFarland slumped into his desk chair. "What's done is done, I suppose. And if you wanted to draw the man out, I suppose from a certain perspective, you couldn't have done much better. Besides the boy and that Slayton woman, I don't believe the sheriff has really attached himself to too many folks here. And our move on that deputy was almost too clean, reckless as it was."

"A woman, you say?" Reese leered. "Well, hell, if I'd've known that, we could've come up with a whole new plan."

McFarland looked at the hired gun, feeling a sneer of disgust tug at the corner of his mouth. "We have certain codes we try to follow here, sir. Not that you seem to have any concern for them."

"If you want someone to follow the rules, you don't call me," Reese said, his face growing grim again. "You brought me here because you had a problem you couldn't solve, and now I'm solving it. Best watch what you're insinuating, or you may have more problems than you bargained for."

"Is that a threat?" McFarland attempted offense, though the waver in his voice belied more than a small amount of concern.

"It's just a fact," Reese said, hitching his thumbs in his belt.

McFarland looked down at the deadly hands. They were lightning quick. He'd seen it himself, and despite the gunslinger's nonchalance, either of the guns on his hips could be drawn and fired before McFarland would have enough time to take a final breath. "Well, there is nothing better for business than facts. I hope in the future you'll have the courtesy to run your plans by me before executing anyone else."

"I told you, he ain't dead."

"I don't know how you can be so sure of that."

"Because I'm the one who shot him," Reese said. "If I wanted him dead, he'd be dead. There's another fact for ya."

McFarland sighed, looking to Anne-Marie for any help, but the woman just continued to watch the exchange.

"Besides," Reese picked up again, "that wasn't necessarily the plan. I was just in there to scare the kid. Figured word'd get back to Rosman. He'd come wanting to hash it out with me, then there ya go. Pure luck the kid chose today to be brave. Hell, you may've saved yourself some bucks on the deal."

"Oh?" McFarland sighed. "And how's that, exactly? You're giving me a discount? Two for one?"

Reese laughed. "No, no. I see you misunderstood yet again. Price for Rosman's one thousand dollars. That ain't changed and ain't gonna. But you didn't think I'm floating here on my own dime, did ya? Man's gotta eat. Man's gotta have entertainment. And that money ain't coming outta my pocket. But the quicker Rosman gets fired up, the quicker he goes down, the quicker I move on, and you don't need to worry about my daily essentials."

McFarland looked to Anne-Marie again.

Finally, the woman spoke up, a broad smile putting her straight white teeth on display. "You pay for the best, Frank.

I'd be thankful he's willing to stay in that slovenly cabin you call a bunkhouse."

Reese looked at the woman and grinned. "You offering better lodgings?"

The woman laughed fully and throatily. "You couldn't afford it, even at Frank's rates."

Reese looked her up and down. "I'll keep that in mind."

"Look," McFarland broke in. "The point is, Rosman is curious now. More than curious, perhaps. But enraged is what we need. We need him to act like a man, not like a sheriff. It's the only way to guarantee we get rid of him. I'm willing to give this the time it takes. Let the dust settle and let him stew. After that, we meet here again and come up with our next steps. Together. Does anyone have a problem with that?"

The three exchanged glances before Reese spoke up. "Just be needing some walking around money, boss."

***

That night, Chancy and Teresa sat at the dining room table. Betsy was between them, diligently working through her arithmetic and times tables.

"He's going to be all right," the girl said, pausing at her work. It was a trait she'd picked up from her mother, that ability to see what others were thinking and feeling. It unnerved Chancy when Teresa did it, but it was downright unsettling when Betsy did.

"I know," the man said. "And I'm grateful for that. But it don't make matters much better."

"Doesn't," the girl said.

"Doesn't make them better." Chancy smiled.

"So what are you going to do?" the girl asked. "Shoot the man?"

"Betsy," Teresa broke in.

"It's only logical, Momma. And the Bible says an eye for an eye."

"Yes," Teresa said, "but perhaps you should study a bit more about what it has to say about forgiveness."

Betsy looked between her mother and Chancy. "Perhaps you should tell him that," the girl said.

"All right." Teresa leaned across and put her hand on her daughter's. "That's just about enough from you for one evening."

"I've still got to review." Betsy gestured at her papers.

"Then review upstairs. Off you go."

The girl sighed, gathered her materials, and went to the bottom of the steps. She turned back to Chancy. "If you shoot that man," she said, "I'll forgive you. Just like the Bible says. Good night, Mr. Rosman."

"Good *night*, Betsy," Teresa said.

Chancy looked over at the woman as Betsy clomped up the stairs to her room. "She's got a point," he said.

Teresa stood and started gathering their cups from an evening tea. "Oh, I'm quite aware of that," she said. "But I'll thank you to not let her know that."

"She's gotta grow up sometime."

"Is that what you told Andy's father?"

Chancy clenched his jaw. The woman knew how to sting him. "Listen," Chancy said. "What's going on here. It's getting out of hand. What happened before, yeah, it kept me busy, and it kept folks spooked, but this is a line you don't cross. If a bunch of rabble is going after one another, all right. But that boy didn't have no part in it."

"Oh? I thought he was your partner."

"Now look," Chancy stood up. "Maybe I was wrong to ask for his help. Maybe I should've kept my distance from him, you, everybody. But I can't undo what's been done. Not with Andy, not with Whittaker. Nobody. But I can try to keep it from happening again."

"And you've got a plan for that, I suppose?"

"I do. You and Betsy gather up your things and get out of here till this blows over. Ain't no secret I've been staying here, even less of one that you and me's become close. Way I figure, if they don't mind going after Andy, they ain't gonna mind going after you two."

"I appreciate your candor and chivalry," the woman said, "but I think you seem to lack a touch of reality. Where exactly is it you expect us to go? And with what money? What happens while we're gone? We can't all just blow away with the wind, Sheriff Rosman."

The words hurt. Not her logic. She was more than right there. But the use of his surname. That hadn't happened since the first few days he'd been staying there.

He sighed, looking down at his hands. "Look, Teresa, I know I'm bringing trouble about with me. That's all I'm getting at. If I thought staying somewhere else would solve that problem, I'd be up there packing my bags right now. But what happened to Andy today, makes things pretty clear. It don't matter where I am, so long as I'm talking to somebody, that person ain't exactly safe."

"Well, then…" Teresa paused in the doorway to the kitchen. "It sounds like there's no sense in us, or you, going anywhere. But there's something you need to know right now, Chancy Rosman. If trouble is following you about, and I can't say I disagree with you about that, there is only one thing for you to do. If you love us, if you love this town, if you love anything, you are honor bound to find this trouble and shoot it dead."

"What about forgiveness?" He looked up at her, smiling. "You changing your mind about that Bible already?"

"Not at all," Teresa said, her eyes cold. "Ecclesiastes chapter three, verse three, Chancy. 'There is a time to kill.'"

Chapter 10
An Evil Plan

The light was dim in the bunkhouse, but even the shade could do little to relieve the stifling midday heat. Frank opened the windows on either side of the door, allowing a faint hint of breeze into the dirty room.

The air was still and thick, and it was taking on an aroma from too many bodies over too many days. While all the men were rarely there at once, and many had found better places to spend their nights, the constant influx of the outlaws had left its own fetid aroma in the air.

This day, only one man sat back in the corner, hiding from the sunlight, stretched out on a bunk with his hat down over his eyes.

"Come up here where I can see you," Frank said. "We need to talk."

Reese tipped his hat up slightly, as if to verify the identity of the man who addressed him. Then, at an almost purposefully sluggish pace, he swung his legs to the floor, his boots hitting the wood with a solid thunk.

Reese twisted his head back and forth, cracking the vertebrae in his neck, adjusted his belt, and took his time wandering up to the wooden table at the front of the room.

"Can't say as I really care for the tone of your voice there, feller," he said.

"Well, I can't really say as I care for the way things have been going on your side, either," McFarland said. "I was against this whole thing with the boy, but you've been reassuring me it would draw Rosman out. Well, it's been two days now and"—McFarland looked theatrically around the room—"I don't see any sheriff. In fact, if I'm not mistaken, I've had more to do with him than you have."

"Told ya, I needed to get a lay of the land to plan my moves. Had to get a feel for the man."

"Yes, well, I'm thinking this has become a bit more of a vacation for you than I was led to believe it would be."

"Hey, you know I can take him. Say the word, I'll saddle up, and he'll be dead in the hour. But I thought you wanted some finesse in this."

McFarland sighed. "Yes, you're right. But patience is not one of my virtues, I'm afraid, and this man has pushed me to my limit. If I'd known this was going to be your way of handling things, I'd've gone about it much differently."

"Now there's your problem, Frank." Reese smiled across the table. "You sit there thinking everything's gotta be done just so. That everything has a way to be handled. And maybe that's true for you, what with your papers and your businesses and your little schemes, but from this side of things, solutions are much simpler."

"You can't just shoot the man. It would bring everything down on my head."

"That's right." Reese grinned. "On your head."

"And you don't think they'd figure out who you were working for?"

Reese glared at him.

"Working with," McFarland quickly amended.

"Seems to me," Reese said, "a man in your position oughtta think a little more before he talks. In some places, a feller like me might take what you just said as a threat. And I know you ain't figuring to threaten a feller like me."

McFarland sighed again. "No, no, Mr. Reese. It was not a threat. Think of it more as an assessment of facts. I'm not foolish enough to think I've pulled the wool over everyone's eyes. And to be quite honest with you, that has never been my intention. I only need to pull the wool over some eyes, convince *some* people I'm on their side, and by then, the paperwork is on my side, and it doesn't matter who has or has not been fooled. Once contracts are signed, affairs take a much more complex order. At least, that's how it's usually been."

"Yeah, well, now it ain't," the gunslinger said, leaning back in his chair.

"No," Frank mused. "No, it isn't. Which is why I'm here. A person of your experiences and, um, complexities would likely approach this situation in a manner somewhat different from me. And while I appreciate your creativity with the Nichols boy, I don't think that's precisely the direction I'd like to see things going."

"You said to get the sheriff riled. Ain't my fault he don't seem to care much for that boy."

"Oh, he cares," McFarland said. "He's been down visiting two times a day. The problem is Rosman is smart. In some ways, I believe your plan worked too well."

Reese laughed. "Now that'll be the first time a feller got on me for being too good."

"Our previous sheriff would've taken the bait, hook, line, and sinker. But he wasn't a man we had to worry about to begin with. The problem with Rosman is he knows exactly what you're trying to do, and he won't play into our hands."

"Too good," Reese muttered to himself again, smiling.

"Yes, too good. While there may be some gray area in here you said the boy asked you to leave, so technically you would've been trespassing, Rosman knows that's a small fish to fry. And what I'd just about bet on is he knows you aren't worth something as piddly as that day in court."

"Not worth it, huh?" Reese raised an eyebrow.

"Indeed. Why bother with something that we'd just bail you out for, anyway? You say it was self-defense, the sheriff says it was aggression, we go back and forth. Odds are the court sees it his way. But, no, if you ask me, I'd say that man wants to see you hang."

Reese smiled. "I could sell tickets to that show."

"I've no doubt," McFarland said. "But the point is he will not act unless one of two things happens. Either he gets enough on you or me to make his move, or we take a more drastic step and force him to."

"You're kinda tying my hands here, Frank. You tell me to make a move, I do, and then you ride me for it. Tell me it's too good and then that it ain't good enough. Maybe you can have it both ways in your meetings with the big boys, but I don't cotton much to—how'd you put it?—the complexities. You want me to do something, you tell me, I do it. That's how I work. The rest of it, well, that all falls in your lap."

"Yes, yes," McFarland said. "I understand that. But I'm here for… Well, I guess I'm here for advice. You're a man of action. What are your thoughts?"

"Outside of just shooting the man and being done with it?"

"Preferably, yes." McFarland paused. "But let's not entirely forget that idea, should it come to it."

Reese laughed. "You boys're always making things more difficult than they gotta be. But all right. If we can't shoot him, and he ain't reacting to the deputy or the boy, well, I say we just push a little harder. Who else's he keen on in this town?"

"Oh, he's fairly popular with most folks," McFarland said. "Really seems to have taken a liking to the town, and they to him."

"Sure, but if he ain't moving on the kid, he ain't gonna get too riled up if we pop ol' Jennings at the saloon neither. There's gotta be somebody, Frank. Use your head. You're not gonna make me do all the work, surely."

Frank looked up at the ceiling, brushing away an errant fly. Slowly, a small grin spread across his face. "The woman."

Reese grinned. "Bingo."

"The landlady," McFarland continued, a slight look of concern on his face. "We don't hurt her. We don't harm her in any way. But we just, well… We just take her."

"A kidnapping, huh?"

"Well, I suppose with an adult, it would technically be an abduction."

"Whatever you wanna call it, it's all the same to me."

"It's perfect. With the boy, Rosman knows he's technically safe. Yes, he's got some healing to do, but he's home. The sheriff can check in on him. Keep an eye on things. But if Mrs. Slayton just vanishes…"

Reese's smile matched his employer's. "Yeah, I reckon that'd drive him straight batty."

"How long would it take you to arrange something?"

Reese shrugged. "Not much time at all, depending on how you wanna do it. Hell, you want a little spectacle? I can head out now."

"No, no," McFarland said. "We can't be too grandiose here. Naturally, Rosman will assume you and I are involved, but we don't want it to be too clear. Otherwise, he'll have us both sitting in that rotten jail of his."

"That gal of yours'll get us out in no time."

McFarland chewed on it. "True, but we need this to be clean. It's one thing if he suspects we are involved. It's another if he sees someone and can prove it. With this, we want her to just… poof!" He gestured in the air. "Suddenly be unaccounted for."

"Maybe," Reese said. "Maybe you got a point. But I bet ya we can meet in the middle here."

"I'm listening."

***

Just as Chancy was settling his affairs for the evening in the office, thinking longingly of a warm meal and an evening on the porch, the door to the station flew open.

Betsy, usually reserved if somewhat ornery, burst into the room. "Chancy! You've got to do something! It's bad! I don't know what to do!"

"Whoa." Chancy patted the air in front of him. "Slow down, Bets. Slow down. Talk to me now. What's going on?"

"Momma!"

Immediately, Chancy's face darkened. His hand unconsciously went to the butt of his gun. "What do you mean? Tell me exactly."

"Exactly?" The girl's temper flared momentarily, but she caught herself. "Exactly what happened is something I don't know. I can tell you what has happened, and that is nothing. Momma is nowhere. Not at the house, not at the store. Never, never does she go somewhere without telling me. Or at least leaving a note. Chancy, she's just gone!"

Chancy felt his nerves settle, but only slightly. The fact someone as responsible as Teresa Slayton would ever act unusually, especially with her daughter involved, was more than concerning. But at least as of yet, there was nothing to panic about.

That was the only surefire way to ruin things before they got started. "All right, Betsy, I want you to just tell me what you know. Simple, right?"

The girl sighed, flounced into the chair across from him, and looked up at the sheriff. "That's the problem, Chancy. I know nothing! She's just gone!"

"We don't wanna jump to conclusions, though, all right?"

"No?" the girl's voice raised again. "You think I don't see what's going on in this town? Ever since you became sheriff, it's been nothing but trouble. First Mr. Whittaker, then Andy, and now Momma. You think I don't know what's going on just because I'm a kid, but it sure looks like it don't pay to be your friend."

For the briefest moment, Chancy thought of correcting her. The girl, like her mother, was constantly pointing out his errors in speech. But he knew, if anything was a true sign of distress in the girl, it was this. "You might be right, kid, but that's not here or there right now. We're in the mud, so let's figure out what to do about it. When was the last time you saw her? This morning?"

"Lunch," Betsy said, looking down at her wringing hands. "No, wait. I saw her out the window this afternoon. That's why I thought she'd be at the mercantile."

"Okay," Chancy said, trying to use a soothing tone. "That's good. So you were still in school then. About what time you think it was?"

"Oh, I don't know!" the girl cried out. "Why are we sitting here? Why don't you just go find her? This is your fault!"

Chancy started to respond, then waited. The girl had a point, maybe even more than she realized. And if there was one thing he'd learned about Betsy Slayton, it was never to underestimate her by her age. He gave her a few moments to gather herself.

"I'm sorry," the girl finally said.

"It's all right," Chancy replied. "You might darn well be right. But like I said..."

"Yeah, yeah. We're in the mud." Betsy stared down at her hands for a moment. "It must've been about three. Maybe a little after. We were almost done for the day. We were going over our arithmetic, and, well..."

"You were daydreaming. I understand. I keep telling that teacher you're too clever for that class."

The girl smiled almost imperceptibly. "It's pretty easy."

"And you're smart as a whip. So it's about three, you look out the window and see your ma heading into town. She seemed okay? Not rushing or anything?"

"She's always rushing," the girl said, a slight hitch in her voice as she fought to control her emotions. "But no. Or yes, I guess. She seemed normal. I don't know for sure she was going to Andy's, but she was headed that direction, and that's just my guess."

"I reckon you already talked to Andy?"

"Of course I already talked to Andy," Betsy said. "I went home after school, straight home, and didn't see her. But I assumed she was out doing chores, or not back yet, or—oh, I don't know. But after a while, I wondered. I worried, really. So I looked around the place and didn't see any sign of her. And as I said, she never leaves me alone without telling me where she'll be. So I asked the neighbors. They were no help, of course. And then I came into town, and Andy hasn't seen her. I looked at the restaurant. I even looked in the saloon, Chancy! She's just gone!" The girl's shoulders shook as her emotions grew too big for her. Tears spilled over and ran down her cheeks.

"She's gone, Chancy! She could be anywhere! She could be hurt! And I don't know how to help her!"

Chancy walked around the desk and stood the girl up by the shoulders. She tried to shrug his hands off, but he held her firmly, wanting her to have the reassurance of another person, wanting her to work through her emotions.

When she'd caught her breath, she wiped at her eyes and looked up at the man. "Thank you for not hugging me. I'm not a child."

"I know you ain't," Chancy said.

"Aren't," the girl said, almost automatically.

Inwardly, Chancy smiled. This was the girl he needed. "All right, Bets, listen up. Here's the plan. I need you to go up and holler at the mayor. Anybody give you any flack, tell 'em you're on official business from the sheriff. Have him gather up any men in town he trusts and have 'em meet me down at the mercantile. You see anybody you know on your way, tell 'em the same."

"I already checked there," Betsy said, her voice raising slightly again.

"I know you did," Chancy said calmly. "It's just as good a meeting place as any. You round up some folks, tell 'em to move quick fast, and I'll be there waiting. No lollygagging."

"Okay." The girl seemed to firm up some under the responsibility. "And then?"

"And then we go over every inch of this town till we find your momma. Now get going."

The girl turned and raced out, the door banging behind her. Chancy adjusted his hat, checked his revolver, and rubbed at the back of his neck. If this is how they wanted things to go, then it was time the gloves came off.

***

Every town holds its secrets, some more closely than others. Elkhorn was no different. Despite the group of eager volunteers who had met Chancy at the mercantile... despite checking and rechecking stories, stables, and bunkhouses...

despite Chancy himself spending another two hours scouring the town long after dark had settled in and his volunteers had gone home to rest, their efforts had brought about no information.

It was as if the woman had simply vanished, like she'd never existed at all.

Chancy took the Appaloosa to the small stable behind the boarding house, removing the saddle, brushing her down, and getting some oats and hay for the night.

Betsy had volunteered to stay with Andy's family overnight, supposedly to help with his recovery, but more likely, Chancy thought, to put some distance between herself and the sheriff.

It almost hurt. She was his connection to Teresa. She was the only clue he had, the last person to have seen her that day. But in his heart, he couldn't blame the child.

Life hadn't hardened her yet. Everything she'd gone through in her short time on Earth had given her thick skin, but inside, she was still a little girl.

He couldn't—wouldn't—ask her to stay. Wouldn't put her in the danger of being around him. For all he knew, this was just the beginning.

He'd pulled Mr. Nichols aside before leaving, making sure the man had his rifle loaded and ready. "I don't mean to scare you," Chancy had told the man, "but I'm not gonna blow smoke either. This may get worse before it gets better."

The mercantile owner had looked at him with cold eyes. "Sheriff Rosman, after what happened to my boy, you better hope these fellers come after you before they come to me."

Chancy had nodded. The anger was good. Betsy, at least, was one thing he didn't need to worry about. At least not too much.

He sauntered around the corner of the house from the stable, tired mentally as much as physically. The windows, for the first time he could remember, were dark.

He paused for a moment, listening to the silence, wondering if anyone was waiting inside. His hand crept down to the gun on his hip as he tiptoed across the wooden porch. It was then he saw it.

The paper fluttered in a soft night breeze, tugging slightly at the nail that secured it to the front door. Chancy paused for a moment, reading, then tore the sheet down and crumpled it into a ball, shoving it in the pocket of his jeans.

Whatever these men thought they were doing, they'd just given him the one thing they never should have: opportunity.

"If you want her back," the note read in a scrawled, barely legible hand, "send the sheriff, ALONE, to the shack at Blind Bluff. Saturday. Noon."

It was close to the witching hour by then on Friday night. Chancy entered the house, slamming the door behind him. In twelve hours, they would settle this.

Chapter 11
Taking Back the Town

The next morning, Chancy was awake with the sun. He knew he'd need his wits about him, but he also knew there was no way he could rest until he had Teresa safely back at home and the men responsible for her disappearance, either in jail or in pine boxes.

As he paced the rooms in the boarding house, he realized he was caring less about which of those it was.

Unable to keep his nervous energy in check, he saddled the Appaloosa earlier than he intended and headed for the mayor's house. Maybe it would be more respectful to meet the man in his office.

Surely there was more than enough time to let the mayor know of his plans, but Chancy was tired. Tired of the stress. Tired of waiting. Tired of feeling like he was sitting on his hands.

At least meeting with Mayor Travis was something he could do.

To Chancy' surprise, just as he raised his hand to knock on the mayor's door, the door opened and the man himself stepped out.

"Chancy!" Travis stepped back a bit, surprised. "I was just coming to find you."

"Why? What've you heard?"

"Come inside." The mayor stepped back and gestured the sheriff in.

Taking a place at the dining room table, Chancy swirled a cup of coffee in front of him. The mug was pristine, the highest quality. Not for the first time, a whisper of doubt came to the back of his mind.

The mayor had always seemed reliable, but still... with someone like McFarland around, one never knew who to trust.

Travis folded his hands on the table in front of himself and looked at Chancy. "I assume you must have news to be here so early in the morning."

Chancy looked at the man, assessing him. "So, should I assume the same about you? Seeing as how you were off to find me?"

"No. Well, not really news. I was coming to tell you I was going to round up the men and meet you at the mercantile again first thing this morning. It was my guess you'd want to be out searching as soon as possible, and I didn't want to miss you."

"That's all?"

"That's all," the mayor said. "What is It, Chancy? There's something you're not telling me."

Chancy looked around the immaculate room, down at his coffee mug again. "You do all right being mayor and all, huh?"

"Well, it's a..." The mayor trailed off. "Oh. Oh, I see. Chancy, none of this is mine, any more than the bed you sleep in is yours. This is the mayor's home, to be sure, but only mine, so to speak, as long as I'm mayor."

"Thought they only did that for the president."

"Not everywhere does. Elkhorn just happens to, for the moment at least. Once my term is over, assuming I don't pursue reelection, I'll move out."

"And there wouldn't happen to be a nice ranch waiting for you after all that?"

"Sheriff Rosman…" The mayor's tone grew stern. "What's waiting for me after this happens to be a nice ranch, as a matter of fact. The same ranch that's been in my family for three generations. Now, I can appreciate you're under a lot of stress, and I know as well as anyone the backroom deals that go on in this town, but I assure you, what you're thinking right now could not be farther from the truth."

"So you're telling me your pockets aren't being lined?"

"I'll forgive the insult, given the circumstances, but I'll warn you to never make it again."

Chancy eyed the man. The mayor's look was calm, if offended, but direct and honest. "All right," Chancy said. "I just needed to know."

"As I said," Travis continued, "I understand. But rather than start going after one another, which I'm sure would be more than our common enemy could hope for, perhaps we should get down to solving this problem. Mr. Nichols has been in my office every day this week asking when I'm going to bring in the man who shot his son. Now, one of the finest citizens we have has gone missing and left her daughter at the mercy of the town. A line has been crossed, one that I should've been defending all along.

"I won't sit here and tell you I've always made the right choices. I've done what I thought was best in the moment, and it's landed us here. I'm prepared to take my share of the blame for that, but bemoaning it at the present time will not get us any closer to finding Teresa Slayton."

Chancy reached in his pocket and pulled out the paper, smoothing it on the white tablecloth before handing it over to the mayor. "I know where she is, or at least where we're supposed to start."

The mayor looked down at the page, reading the brief message, then looking back up at the sheriff. "You realize..."

"Yeah," Chancy said. "That's an invitation to an execution if I ever saw one. Thing is... I don't see a lot of options. And if it gets that girl her momma back, well, I intend to keep that appointment."

"Oh, you'll keep the appointment, Sheriff Rosman. I'll be the last person to talk you out of that. But alone? I think not."

Chancy sighed. "I figured you'd say something like that. To be honest, I don't know if I came here because I knew you would or because I hoped you'd try to talk me out of it. But I don't see any way around it at this point. Worst-case scenario, you'll have another dead sheriff on your hands. Maybe this time you'll bring the fellas in, though."

The mayor paused at the insinuation, then waved it away. "Now's not the time for being foreboding either. What we need is a plan. Obviously, you'll be at Blind Bluff at noon. We can't avoid that, but we can prepare for it. Perhaps this will be the one mistake this gang has made so far."

"What's that?" Chancy asked.

"Giving us time to plan." The mayor leaned back in his chair, fingering the page. "Here's what I think. You came to me to at least inform me of your plans, which I appreciate. I'd like to make a counter-offer. Let's follow along with my plan. Our search party will meet at the mercantile in about twenty minutes. Come with me and let's see what happens once we spread this new bit of information. You'll still have more than enough time to ride off to this shack"—he spat the word—"if you insist on doing so on your own, but I ask that you at least give me this chance before making your decision."

The sheriff looked at the mayor for a moment. "All right," he said finally. "Let's go see who's shown up."

***

Inside the mercantile, twenty men sat, stood, and leaned against various chairs and counters throughout the room. Few were armed, but the tone of the place was deadly serious.

As if to underscore the point, Andy Nichols sat on the wooden counter by the register, his arm hanging in a white linen sling across his body.

At eight o'clock, the mayor stepped forward. "Men," he began, "I want to thank you personally for coming, every one of you. As we are all aware, the past nine months have not been pleasant for our town. Like roaches, criminals have slipped in undercover, setting up nests and striking out with ever-greater brazenness and disregard. Perhaps some of you are thinking I should've done something about this by now, and I'm here to tell you, I agree. But as some of you also know, often, our problems don't present themselves as problems in the beginning. What sounds like a good deal one day can turn sour the next. The stranger you invite to your home for dinner slips out in the night with your valuables. We've all been doing our best to continue hoping that somehow this problem would take care of itself. And I'm no better.

"For that I apologize." Travis gestured to Andy. "But when our children and our women are in danger, that is something we cannot stand for. They say the west is a lawless, dangerous place, that us folks who come out here know what we're getting into. Some even say we deserve it. But that's not what I see here. I see men who care about their community… their families. I see men who are stepping forward to help those in an hour of need. Some of you were with us last night as we scoured this town for Teresa Slayton. Those of you who were know we came back tired and empty-handed.

"There are two things that give me hope, though. One is, as I look around me, I see more faces than I did last evening. Word has spread, and despite what others might think about this wild country we inhabit, more men have shown themselves worthy and honorable. To all of you, I offer my deepest thanks and utmost respect. The other thing that gives me hope is that we have news. Sheriff Rosman?" The mayor turned to Chancy and stepped back from the center of the room.

Chancy looked around at the men. A posse they were not, but he saw determination in their faces and a desire to do what was right. "Men," he said, "I ain't much of a speech-giver, so I'll keep this short. Last night when I got back to the boarding house, I found this note on the door." He held up the paper. "This here maybe ain't the answer we were looking for, but it's an answer. I'm to meet up with Miss Slayton's abductors at noon today, out up by Blind Bluff."

There was a murmur in the crowd. The location was known, if only by reputation, to most of the men in the town. It was a desolate place, wind-blown and nearly barren.

"Now, the mayor and I've been kicking around the best way to go about that. Ya see, this here note is pretty darn specific that I come on my own, and that's just what I intend to do."

The voices in the crowd raised clear protestations.

"If," the mayor broke in, stepping forward, "we don't come up with a better plan. I, for one, am not keen on losing another sheriff."

"Specially one that's actually doin' the job!" a voice called out.

"Yes," the mayor said. "Especially because of that. But also because we are not a town of men who will sit back and let others sacrifice for us. When there is a problem in this town, it is all of our problem. When one of ours is hurt, in need, missing, it is not a problem for a few close friends or relatives. It is a call to us to stand up and do what's right.

"Initially, I asked you all here to help us search for Teresa Slayton. It would appear now that aspect of our job has been resolved. Assuming the captive and the captors are in the same place—"

"Ain't nowhere else we didn't look," a man said.

"Precisely," the mayor said. "Given the information we have and the work we've put in, I believe Mrs. Slayton will be found in the shack at Blind Bluff, along with the men who have absconded with her. As I was saying, however, assuming this is true, we have a new set of problems on our hands. We don't know who, or how many men, are out there."

"Ask McFarland," a third voice said, resulting in murmurs of agreement from around the room.

"McFarland will have his day," the mayor said, "once we can prove his involvement."

A general sigh was heard. The town had been listening to the same story for too long. McFarland's schemes were too slick, his papers were always in order, and his plans were always a few steps ahead. Proving the man had done something illegal was like pouring water uphill, it simply couldn't be done.

"How 'bout you just hang back here and let us go solve this one for ya, Mayor?" a voice called.

"Any of you does that, and I'll be coming for you next," Chancy said, stepping forward to the center of the crowd. "That's something y'all need to put out of your heads right now. You wanted me as sheriff. Well, all right, you got me. But I'm telling you right now, long as I'm the law, we're going along with the mayor. At least..." Chancy grinned ever-so-slightly. "'Less something comes up otherwise." Chancy simply shrugged when Mayor Travis shot a glance at him. "Man wants a gunfight. He better be prepared for bullets."

"What we are aiming for," the mayor said, "is bringing these men in alive. These men, whoever they may be. Once we've done that, we let the law do its job."

A slight grumble of discontent wended its way around the room.

"Fact is," Chancy said, "we don't know what we're walking into. One thing I know is Teresa Slayton's gonna be in the middle of it. So all you with itchy fingers best keep that in mind."

"Well, what're we standing around chawin' for?" A man stepped out of the crowd—Andy's father. His rifle was gripped tightly in his hands, his knuckles white. "You know where the men who did this to my boy are. I'd like to go have a word with 'em."

Chancy pressed the air in front of him. "That brings me to my next point." He looked around the room. "I wanna join the mayor here in saying how much I 'ppreciate y'all coming out here. But, safe to say, every one of you thought you were signing up for a search party, not a shootout."

"Sounds even better, you ask me," Mr. Nichols said.

"Well, sir…" Chancy looked over. "I ain't asking you. Fact, lemme see that gun for a second."

Mr. Nichols looked at him and then slowly handed the rifle over.

"Much obliged," Chancy said. "Now that you're unarmed, I'm gonna give you, give all of you, some ground rules. And rule number one: you got a wife, you got kids, you ain't going."

Cries burst up around the room.

Andy's father took a step forward but, meeting Chancy's glare, hesitated, then stepped back. "That ain't right," Mr. Nichols said. "I got more at stake in this game than any of the rest of these men."

"I know ya do," Chancy said. "And I know not only have you got your own kin to look after, you got Teresa's girl at your house now as well. You wind up dead. Who you planning on taking over for ya?"

Mr. Nichols protested but, seeing his defeat, punched his fist into his palm. "You expect me to just sit back and do nothing?"

"I expect you to listen," Chancy said calmly. "This is how it's gonna be. You can like it or not like it, but you better start accepting it now." He held Mr. Nichols's gaze a moment longer, then tossed the gun back to him. "We're divvying y'all up. Raise your hand if you got kin, a wife, anything like that." Chancy looked across the room as roughly half the hands went up. "That's 'bout what I expected. You men are staying in town, not cause we don't want ya, but because we're hoping we don't need you.

"You sit and think for a minute instead of popping off. You might realize what the mayor told me afore we came in here. You take a town full to the brim with lowlifes and you tell 'em the sheriff and every able-bodied man is gonna be out in the boondocks at noon. What do you think's gonna happen?" He looked around. "Yep, you got it. All hell's gonna break loose. You boys are here to make sure we got a safe place to bring this woman back to. I ain't keen on risking my skin to go out there and get her, just to catch a bullet when I walk back into town."

There were sounds of agreement from the crowd, if not enthusiastic ones.

"So listen," Chancy said. "Y'all's half are gonna be our guard in the town. You other fellas, we got a new plan for you, so pay attention." He glanced back at the mayor.

"This is what we need," Travis started. "All of you, when we leave here, are to go to your homes, arm yourselves. Those with loved ones get them to a safe place. Out of town if you can, but given the short notice here, I'm afraid we're almost all going to improvise. I sincerely hope things will remain quiet until we return, but if not, the last thing I want is for any of us to be caught unaware. This is serious enough already. Let's not let it get any worse.

"Those of you who will ride out with us, I'm going to split you up." The mayor, familiar with his citizens, began moving the men into groups, the half with family responsibilities to one side, the rest in two groups of five. "Right now, it's"—he checked his pocket watch—"nearly nine. Chancy is going to keep his appointment for twelve noon, precisely. That gives us three hours. Blind Bluff is about an hour's ride from here, so I want you to go home, get your guns, arrange your affairs if need be, and be prepared to leave in one hour. Half of you will come in from the east, the other half from the west. Chancy will ride straight up from the south. By the time he arrives, I expect all of you to have found cover and be settled in well ahead of time.

"It's safe to assume Frank McFarland is no slouch, as we've all experienced, so in no case shall you ride out as a group. We should see no more than two men leaving in any direction at any one time. I'll leave it to you to decide who goes when and where, but your instructions are as stated. Be in position by eleven o'clock. No later.

"When Sheriff Rosman arrives, you're to stay as you are. Be close enough you can see him clearly, and pay close attention. He will run things from that point forward. Do not be heroes. Do not go after Teresa before Chancy is there. Do nothing without Chancy saying so first. If we play our cards right, we might pull this off without firing a shot."

Chancy glanced over at the mayor, eyebrow raised.

"I'm not saying it's likely," Travis said. He looked back at the men in the shop. "Now's our time to take this town back. We've all got jobs to do. Let's go do them."

As the men filed out of the shop, conversing in groups of two and three, Chancy pulled the mayor to the side. "I gotta give it to ya, Mayor. You can give one fine speech."

Travis looked up at him. "I need to go get my affairs in order," he said and walked out the door, leaving Chancy to stare after him.

Chapter 12
The Showdown

It was just before noon when Chancy rode slowly up toward the cabin. His days as a bounty hunter could sometimes feel so far behind him, but moments like these, willingly putting himself into the nest of rattlesnakes, always brought those feelings back.

His senses were heightened.

The soft breeze coming across the flat land formed small dust whirls around him. The sounds of his horse's hooves were the only ones to reach his ears.

Not a bird chirped. In the distance, he could make out the shack, a weather-beaten, decrepit building that hadn't housed a soul—at least not a law-abiding one—in years. Outside it, they tethered a pair of horses to a worn-out hitching post.

He wanted to believe he was approaching two, maybe even one, outlaw. But the odds they had given Teresa a horse, as opposed to simply tying her hands and dumping her over a saddle, were low. Even then, two horses were a feeble attempt to allay his fears.

Two horses meant two men, at least, were in the cabin. But how many more were tucked away in the surrounding scrub and underbrush? How many made a wide circuit walking what they hoped would soon be a killing ground?

Chancy strained his ears for any other sounds of motion or voices, the whicker of a horse that might tell him if the mayor's men had been apprehended already. Was he making his way into not one, but two ambushes: the one for him, the others for those who thought they were getting the jump on him?

The silence, he hoped, was a good sign. But he also knew that, between his men and McFarland's, the chance for crossfire was high.

He needed to move smoothly and quickly, or he and Teresa both might end up at the wrong end of a stray bullet.

About twenty feet from the door to the shack, he stopped, pulling a bandana from his pocket. Removing his hat, he wiped his forehead and around his eyes. He needed clear vision for whatever was about to go down.

He wiped his palms, removing any slippery stray sweat brought on by the midday heat. Stuffing the cloth back in his pocket, he breathed in slowly.

The moisture wasn't from nerves nor from any anxiety. The feeling of calm had settled over him, as it always did when he was preparing to confront his potential demise.

In these moments, very few things mattered, and one above all: speed. Speed of mind almost more than speed of hand. Chancy had been in enough showdowns to know, more than anything, they often came down to luck. It wasn't something he liked, but it was something he had accepted long ago.

He wanted to look for the other men, get some kind of bearing on his situation, find escape routes, assess potential danger areas, but he knew the more he looked, the more time he wasted and, most importantly, the more he might give away.

He slipped his boot out of the stirrup, stepping down off the horse, keeping his hands out from his body, just below chest height. They were far enough away from his guns to fool most folks, but the man he'd seen shoot Andy would know better. Chancy had to hope.

He cleared his throat. "All right," Chancy hollered. "I'm here! Show me the woman!"

Slowly, the door to the shack creaked open. It was dark inside. The high-noon sun made it nearly impossible to distinguish anything in the shadows. Another of their ploys, he thought. The men in the cabin would look out from the dark, their vision much more adapted to the target he created than his to them.

"Keep your hands up," a voice called from the door. "But maybe just a little higher, why don't you?"

Chancy sighed. He knew the voice immediately. He raised his hands to shoulder height and waited.

From the darkness, forms emerged. First Teresa with her hands behind her back, still bound no doubt. Then, behind her, barely visible behind the human barrier, Chancy could just make out the face of Daniel Reese.

Reese had one arm around Teresa's neck, the other nudged her forward from behind. Chancy knew he was jamming a revolver into her back, encouraging her hesitant steps. He made eye contact with her briefly.

She appeared uninjured. Her hair was in shambles and her dress was torn across one shoulder, but there were no signs of violence otherwise. For the moment, that was all he needed to know. The woman could walk and, presumably, run. That would be her only job if things went right.

"You know, we had a wager," Reese said, his grin just visible over the woman's shoulder. "Some of the boys didn't think you'd show."

"And you?" Chancy asked, biding his time, looking for angles.

"Oh, I knowed you'd come around sooner or later. But I gotta be honest," Reese laughed. "I figured the boy'd be the one to get you riled. Should've known you was more of a ladies-type man."

"I'd hate to disappoint you," Chancy said. "How much did you win?"

Reese laughed again. "Oh, it ain't about the money. I got plenty of that coming to me real soon. More about the pride, you know what I mean? I don't like to be wrong. Don't like to look foolish. I got you pegged as about the same way, which—don't you just feel kinda foolish right now? I mean, what's your plan here, Sheriff? You wanting me to just hand her over, say I'm sorry?"

Chancy took another slow breath. He'd been prepared for the taunting, prepared for the arrangement. No fool would walk out without some kind of protection. It was how men like Reese survived.

Sure, the stories might tell otherwise, but in the end, they were all selfish, cowardly opportunists, ready to sacrifice any life to save their own. And now it was Teresa's in the balance.

"Not much to say, huh?" Reese continued to taunt him. "You wanting to just come out here and have a real showdown, I bet? See who's the better man, who's the fastest gun, all that? Well, I hate to tell ya..." Reese moved his arm from behind Teresa's back, reaching over her shoulder to point the revolver at Chancy. "I don't really give two damns about them types of things. You know what matters to me? Walking outta here alive. Well, that and riding out of town with my fee."

"How much you makin' on this job?" Chancy watched the man's hand. It was steady, unwavering. For the moment, all of Reese's attention was on Chancy.

Reese laughed. "Wantin' to know what the price on your head is, are ya? Well, I can't fault a man for that. I tell ya, you can die proud, son. McFarland's got a cool thousand bucks waiting on me, soon as I get back to the old bunkhouse."

"You think you can trust him?"

"I think if I can't, you won't be the only body I drop today."

Chancy looked around slightly, seeking signs of movement. To his left were some small boulders, an old watering trough in front of them. To his right was a bit of scrub, some sickly trees attempting to survive in the empty land.

"You ready to watch your feller die?" Reese said to Teresa, which was followed by the unmistakable sound of a cocking revolver.

Chancy was fast, he knew that, but the man had the drop on him. He could hope for a bad aim or a misfire. He could get down and fire from a kneeling stance. But none of these things removed Teresa from danger. He looked back up at Reese.

A shot rang out loud, cracking off to Chancy's right. A handgun didn't give a report like that.

Reese turned quickly, sweeping his gun toward the direction of the fire in an ingrained, almost instinctive motion to defend himself.

In that brief split second, Chancy saw his moment. Teresa had spun away from Reese, taking advantage of the man's movement. Reese, if only for an instant, seemed to realize his mistake.

Chancy fired from the hip, relying on his instinct rather than his eye. The bullet tore through the air, bursting into the front of Reese's throat before exploding out the back. The man clutched at the wound, shock and momentary disbelief flashing across his eyes as his knees weakened. He staggered once, then fell to his knees, keeling over to the side.

"Go!" Chancy shouted to the woman. "To the rocks! Get down!"

She was a bright woman, perhaps the smartest he'd ever met, but even in that moment, her initial reaction could've gotten her killed.

She'd started toward Chancy, then at his order, and realizing the danger of being close to him, she diverted toward the safety of the rocks, diving to the ground as gunfire rang out around them.

Chancy didn't have time to think, couldn't wonder if the fire was from friend or foe. He darted toward the trees, hitting the dirt at full speed as bullets tore through the leaves and branches above him.

Bullets kicked up dust around him and ricocheted off the rocks by Teresa. Wherever the mayor's men were, he hoped it was close. Chancy cocked his revolver, risking a glance above cover but knowing it was useless.

If the men were firing rifles, which judging by the sound, they undoubtedly were, he would be no match for their range or accuracy with his six-shooter.

Still, he rose briefly, firing high in the general direction of the shots coming his way. His only real goal was to keep Teresa out of danger and the focus on his own pathetic hiding place.

He ventured a look around the trunk of the tree he sat behind. To his left, headed toward Teresa, he could see the dust plumes of advancing horses and even could dimly make out the silhouettes of the men on their backs.

That seemed to be the direction of the fire, but not of the first shot. He looked to his right. An almost mirror image met his eyes. Puffs of smoke matched the crack of shots as the two parties descended on the small killing field where he and Teresa waited.

He reloaded his weapon as quickly as he could, noticing men coming up from the south, the direction he'd rode in from. Surely, he couldn't have missed them.

McFarland's men had all their strength in numbers, none of it in cunning. He glanced around the tree again, and as he'd suspected, more men were riding in from the north. How many were there? And who were they with?

He looked back at Teresa. One thing was certain, he wasn't about to let that woman die alone out here. He hunkered down, tracked the rhythm of the gunfire, and made his move.

Chancy raced across the space, firing ahead of him, above Teresa, at the oncoming men. He dove into the dirt as bullets kicked up splinters from the old trough above them.

Covering her body with his, and keeping her head low, he tried to see where the most immediate danger lay.

He looked back toward the trees. The first group had nearly reached his previous spot. He paused, rubbed his eyes, and looked again.

Mayor Travis, flanked by two men, raced past the scrub, guns drawn and firing. From the south, Chancy could see another trio of men from town, and from the north, just coming into view, were the remaining five.

That put McFarland's men on the hillside ahead of him. Those, and whoever, was left in the building.

Chancy jumped up as the mayor rode past, signaling the trio from the south toward the shack. Chancy raced ahead, guns out and ready.

He burst through the wooden door as the horses outside skidded to a halt, their riders hitting the ground running.

"Down! Everybody down!" Chancy yelled as the glass in the front windows shattered as gun barrels were shoved through.

Outside, the firing continued, but inside, they could hear only the sound of surrender. Guns hit the floor, men hit their knees, and Chancy stood in the center of it all, breathing deeply, his hands steady.

***

Back outside, Chancy helped Teresa to her feet, untying the rope around her wrists. Other than a few scrapes and bruises, she seemed unharmed.

"That was quite the plan you had there," she said, dusting off her dress. "For a moment, I was convinced we weren't going to make it."

"Yeah," Chancy rubbed the back of his neck. "Well..."

She looked at the man, eyes wide. "Do you mean to tell me—"

Just then, Mayor Travis rode up to the pair. "Everyone okay?" he asked, not dismounting his horse.

"Seems to be," Chancy said, eagerly accepting the distraction. "Had a couple boys hunkered down inside there, but your fellas got them under control." He gestured over to the building where the remaining outlaws stood, heads down, hands tied behind their backs.

"That's good," the mayor said. "We need somebody still capable of talking."

Chancy gestured toward the hillside with his head. "Not much left that way?"

"No, Sheriff, I'm afraid not." The mayor shrugged. "But folks know the west is a dangerous place."

Chancy smiled. "I gotta say, Mayor, I didn't know you had it in you."

"Not bad for a pencil-pusher, eh?" Travis wiped at his brow with a handkerchief. "As far as this situation goes, though, I believe we have things under control. If you would be so kind, I believe there is a young lady waiting for her mother in town."

"You sure it's all right?" Chancy asked, thinking of the reinforcements they'd left behind.

"Way I figure, McFarland would've wanted his best out here dealing with you. I may have lingered and taken care of a few loose ends, so I apologize for my tardiness, but word travels fast in Elkhorn. Turns out there were more than just a handful of folks on our side."

"Betsy?" Teresa pulled at Chancy's arm. "She's okay? Tell me she's all right! The men said they'd left her, but—"

"She's fine." Chancy cradled the woman by the shoulders. "I left her with Mr. Nichols."

"But—"

"Ma'am," the mayor interjected, "there isn't a safer place she could be than under the watch of that man."

"Chancy, come on!" Teresa pulled at his sleeve.

The sheriff looked up at the mayor once more.

"You heard the lady," Travis said.

Epilogue

Two nights later, Chancy sat on the porch of Teresa Slayton's boarding house, the proprietress on his right, Betsy on his left, and Mayor Travis perched on the porch rail ahead of them.

"It is a beautiful sound, isn't it?" the mayor laughed.

"I tell you," Chancy replied, "there was a time the clink of coins in a bounty was the only music to my ears, but you're right. The sound of them cuffs going on old McFarland was something I'm not gonna soon forget."

"So that's it then?" Teresa said. "No bond money, no slippery paper trails? You've got him for good?"

"It's more than difficult to talk your way out of a kidnapping charge," the mayor said. "He'll deny it, of course, has been denying it, but with the men we brought back from the cabin, who have been all too eager to discuss everything in great detail, I don't see any way this man can avoid what he's got coming."

"What about the business deals?" she asked. "Are those still legitimate?"

"Well," Travis said. "That part will take some figuring out. Seems there was one factor we forgot about in all the ruckus."

Chancy looked up. "The woman."

Travis nodded. "The woman. And as best as I can tell, that's all we know about her."

"It was Anne-Marie…" Teresa trailed off, looking up. "I don't know that I ever knew her last name."

"I don't know if you ever knew her first name," Travis said. "She went by Anne-Marie here, but something tells me that was just her Elkhorn name. All this time, we had McFarland pegged as the real slick one, but I'm thinking that woman was pulling his strings all along. He just didn't realize it."

"We can't bring her in, too?" Chancy asked.

"If we could find her? Maybe," Travis said. "But I imagine that's one woman who won't wanna be found for a long time, especially not in this town. Seems she made off with some of the money and papers, burned some others, judging by the ashes we found going through McFarland's office, but if you hadn't seen her in that place with your own eyes, you'd never know she was even there."

"But surely someone knows who she is," Teresa said, baffled. "They've both been in town for ages now."

"That's true," Travis said. "But you think about that. You've been here just as long as she was. How often did you see her out? Who'd you see her pallin' around with? Outside that office, I bet you can't think of two places you've seen her, just goin' about her day like regular folk."

Teresa looked off into the distance. "I don't think there was anything regular about any of them."

"You're right about that," Travis said. "Or at least, almost right. The ones Chancy's got down in the jail, they're all sure regular enough to keep there for quite some time. The law doesn't get too up in arms with certain things, and like I said, we've got a lot more than certain things."

"Sounds like you've got your town back," Chancy said.

"Thanks to you," Travis replied. "Which leads me to my next question. We never officially figured out the term of your sheriff's position. I'd be happy to make this more than a temporary arrangement."

Chancy took off his hat and ran his hand through his hair. "I was wondering if that would come up."

"And what have you decided?"

Chancy looked at those gathered around him. "Well, to be quite honest with you, Mr. Mayor, your little town here has kinda grown on me. I don't see no reason I couldn't stick around a spell."

"Any reason," Betsy said beside him.

Chancy shot her a glance, grinning. "That too."

"Come by my office in the morning, then. We can make it official." Travis hopped off the rail, dusted his pants, and extended a hand to Chancy. "Welcome aboard."

"Hey, before you get carried away now," Chancy said, "I have one question for you."

"Let's hear it," Travis said.

"At the shack, when Reese had drawn down on me, somebody fired. I didn't give any signal and nobody was supposed to take a breath without my say-so."

"Sounds like someone saved your life, if you ask me," Travis said.

"It's just been bothering me," Chancy said. "Orders are orders and all."

Travis grinned, replaced his hat, and walked off into the night. "Perhaps your authority was overridden, Sheriff Rosman. See you in the morning."

Chancy looked at Teresa. "You think?"

The woman smiled. "Come inside, Chancy. We are long overdue for a game of dominoes."

He looked down at Betsy. "Well, come on, kid. You heard the lady. My authority's been overrode."

"Overridden," Betsy laughed.

The End

Thanks for taking the time to read this story. A positive review on Amazon would be appreciated.